BATTLE OF THE HEXES

THE GRAVESTONE MYSTERIES - BOOK TWO

JANE HINCHEY

BAYWOLF PRESS
BP
BAYWOLF PRESS

Battle of the Hexes © 2022 Jane Hinchey

To my dad, who was my everything. I wish you were here to hold this book in your hands.

Holly Day, aka Twitch the Witch, has a target on her back.

When Cody Pendant, a black market occult dealer, is murdered, no-one is surprised. Cody was a fraud and a conman who had ripped off almost everyone he'd ever done business with. When her address is found on his body, Holly is convinced the killer is closing in. On her.

Deciding life is better if you're living, she makes plans. Big plans. Plans such as renovating her house. Baking bread. And exploring exactly why her heart skips more than a beat whenever the sexiest lawman she's ever seen is near.

But first she needs to figure out if Cody's killer is the same supernatural assassin out to get her. Easy, right?

CHAPTER
One

I t was hot. Hotter than the hinges on the gates of Hades. Hotter than Satan's butt crack. Sweat pooled in places I'd rather not think about as I limped my way toward Gravestone's foreshore. Flynn, my rat familiar, perched on my shoulder, one paw clutching my hair for balance at my uneven gait. I'd be glad when my broken foot was healed, and I could give this walking boot the boot. *Har har.* I chuckled to myself at the pun, and Flynn swiveled to give me a look. Probably a look that said, *have you lost your ever-loving mind?* Probably.

Hiding out in Gravestone until the hit on me had been neutralized was not my idea of fun. Forbidden from using my magic and given the alias Holly Day was just as grating. As an SIA agent, I wasn't used to twiddling my thumbs and waiting for someone else to save me. I was a woman of action. An elite soldier fighting bad guys of the paranormal variety. Not the book store clerk playing house I claimed to be.

"Come on," I grumbled, my small bout of humor evaporating beneath the heat of the morning. "Doris said the market is fun. According to her, everyone and their dog sets up a table on the first Saturday of the month and sells their treasures."

Streamers and balloons were attached to light poles, and stands lined both sides of the street, residents busily putting out their wares. I spotted Doris across the street at a booth in front of the general store and crossed to where she was unpacking what appeared to be broken and chipped dinner plates.

"Mornin' Holly." Doris glanced up with a smile, her eyes landing on my rat. "Flynn."

He gave her a salute before launching himself off my shoulder and onto the table holding the broken crockery, gingerly picking his way around the display, whiskers twitching as he made it his mission to sniff every single item. Thankfully, his fur was a subdued gray and white today. For some odd reason, Flynn's fur kept changing color—I figured it was something to do with his shifter magic fighting with the dark magic that had turned him into a rat. The same blast that had broken my foot had turned Flynn into a rat. Flynn had saved us both, but at what cost? Was he destined to be stuck in rat form forever? I felt like a dick for grumbling that I had to sit around and do nothing when he definitely had the short end of the stick. From wolf shifter to rat in one fell swoop.

"What's all this?" I jerked my thumb at the broken plates.

"People come from miles around to attend the market," Doris said, pausing to dab at her brow with a red handkerchief. "Sure is a warm one today. Storms brewing."

I glanced at the gray clouds tinged with purple looming on the horizon, slowly closing in. The humidity had to be sitting at two hundred percent. "What does that have to do with selling broken plates?"

"Mosaics."

"Mosaics?"

"Yes. You know. Where you take broken tiles of different colors and create a pretty pattern or picture. Only instead of tiles, you use plates." She swept her arm along her table as if to say *ta-da!*

I cocked my head. "Much more fragile." A dinner plate was considerably thinner than a bathroom tile.

She grinned. "Exactly!"

"This is quite the collection." She had plates of all colors and patterns, some only half a plate, others completely intact except for a small chip or a hairline crack.

"Been collecting them for oodles. I do the rounds at the end of the market and snatch up a bargain. Vendors don't want to drag home any damaged stock and are happy to sell them to me for a song. Or give 'em to me for free."

"Nice." I nodded. I was impressed. Given the price tags she'd attached, I'd imagine she would reap a tidy profit.

Picking up the milkshake take-out cup balanced

precariously on the edge of a shard of porcelain, she placed her lipstick covered lips around the straw and sucked, her cheeks sinking in, leaving her cheekbones in sharp contrast. She released the straw with a pop and a grin. "Want some?"

"Errr, no thanks. What is it anyway?"

Before she had a chance to answer, Flynn came scampering back, keen to inspect the cup. "No, Flynn," I admonished, scooping him up and ignoring his outraged squeaks. "That's Doris's drink. We have no idea what's in it. Remember those cocktails she made? And how sick you got?" Doris, I'd discovered, usually carted around a bottle of something alcoholic in her purse, and the cocktails she'd made us, while being coffee liquor based, had been lethal.

Flynn stopped chattering, clearly remembering. With a heartfelt sigh, he made his way to my shoulder and sat. "Don't worry, we'll go get something to eat and drink shortly," I assured him. To Doris, I said, "So, where's the best place to grab a bite around here?"

"River's, of course."

"No, I meant here at the market." River's café was farther along the foreshore, just after the pier.

"So do I. River sets up a stall selling funnel cakes. They are, of course, out of this world. Come on, I could use a snack. I'll take you."

I waved her back. "That's okay, I'll find it. You have a booth to man."

"Pft, Bernadette can keep an eye on it for a few

minutes, can't you Bernadette?" She raised her voice so the woman at the table next to Doris's could hear.

"What's that, Doris?" Bernadette Bridge was of the same vintage as Doris. Somewhere in her seventies. Only that's where the similarities ended. While Doris was slim and vertically challenged, Bernadette was a larger build, both in height and width. On her table was a clash of colorful doilies.

"I said, you don't mind keeping an eye on my table for ten minutes, do you?" Doris practically shouted.

"Not at all!" Bernadette beamed at us, the lenses on her glasses so thick you could barely make out her eyes.

"Is she blind?" I asked Doris under my breath.

"Color blind, most definitely." Doris snorted, stepping out from behind her table and linking her arm with mine, urging us forward. "She crochets those doilies by memory without using a pattern, but her yarn choices? Oi!"

"Thanks, Bernadette," I called as we stepped away. "I won't keep her long."

Her reply was lost in the surge of the crowd. The stretch of road had been closed off to traffic, and people young and old meandered from one side of the street to the other, keen to view the dozens of stalls open for business.

"I had no idea there were this many people in Gravestone," I commented, dodging a young boy with ice-cream dripping from the cone in his hand.

"There aren't," Doris said. "Vendors and visitors

come from miles around. The market has become quite well known. They're very popular now."

Color me surprised, but I liked it. I liked it all, from the streamers and balloons to bunting that ordinarily would be flapping in the breeze—if there was one. But today, the air was still. Dead still. Not a rustle of a leaf in the trees, zero movement to dry the sweat beading on my skin. "Surely, it's too hot for such activities?" I grumbled, irritation—and perspiration—making my skin itch.

"Nonsense." Doris waved away my concern. "We're used to the heat. Heck, if we waited for a cool day, we'd never have the market at all. Look, there's River. Yoo-hoo!" Doris waved and darted forward. I followed at a more leisurely pace, my walking boot slowing me down. We won't mention the fact that a seventy-year-old woman was running rings around me. It was embarrassing.

"Hello, ladies." River greeted us with a smile until she saw my face, then her smile dropped. "Oh, Holly, you look like you need a little pick me up."

I barked out a snort laugh. Obviously, I looked a wreck. No doubt my face was as red as it felt, my hair plastered to my scalp on account of the sheer amount of sweat I was currently producing. "Thanks."

"I'm sorry. That was rude," River immediately apologized, and I felt a twinge of remorse for making her feel bad.

With herculean effort, I plastered a smile on my face. "No, it wasn't. I'm a little overheated, and it probably shows." No probably about it. I had no doubts I looked as terrible as I felt.

"I've got just the thing." She reached beneath her table, covered with a red and white checkered cloth, and produced a pitcher. "Iced tea?"

"Yes!" I was tempted to snatch the jug from her and down the entire contents in one mouthful. "Please," I hastily added.

"Wanna think about it for a second?" River laughed and poured me a serving in a dixie cup. "Here you go. And how about a funnel cake? A little sugar and carbs will perk you right up."

"Sure, why not?" I watched, sipping my drink, while she sprinkled powdered sugar on the fresh cakes she'd just removed from the fryer.

A commotion a few stalls down caught our attention. Doris and I watched as a young couple appeared to be arguing with a booth holder. I didn't catch everything they were saying, but a few words reached my ears. Words like *fake, fraud, rip-off,* and *money back.*

"That's Cody Pendant," Doris said, brows drawn. She crossed her arms and shifted her weight from one foot to the other. "He's not local. He comes into town every month to set up shop at the market."

"What's he selling?"

"Antique furniture, occult based bric-à-brac, that type of stuff."

The young man was up in Cody's face, poking him

in the chest. The woman had hold of the man's arm and was trying to hold him back. "Who are they?"

"Beau and Claire Whelan, newlyweds. Got married a few months back."

"You made a big mistake messing with us!" Beau Whelan raged, his anger palpable.

"Babe," his wife, Claire, placed a hand on his back in a soothing gesture. "Leave it. For now."

Beau looked down at her, held her gaze for several seconds before his body relaxed, and he took a step back.

Cody watched the pair, a smirk on his face. He was late fifties, early sixties, with a thick head of white-gray hair, a matching, closely trimmed beard, and heavy frown lines deeply embedded in his face. He was big, six foot plus, and broad. He looked like the type of guy who wouldn't hesitate to punch you in the face and laugh as you lay bleeding.

Doris confirmed my assessment. "Cody Pendant is a douche."

"So I see."

"This isn't over," Claire Whelan said to Cody, her voice scarily calm. I felt a shift in the air, and the hairs on my arms stood on end. Flynn felt it too, his claws digging into my shoulder.

"Whatever, sweetheart." Cody sneered, waving his hand in a *move along* gesture. We watched as Beau and Claire clasped hands and left, both of them casting one last, long glare at Cody before pushing through the crowd that had milled around to watch. With the argument over, the spectators soon drifted away.

"Dad!" A pretty woman with green hair that hung in two braids over her shoulders hurried up to Cody. "Take a break. Go cool off," she admonished, hands on hips. I didn't hear his response as River reminded us we were standing at her stall waiting for our funnel cakes.

"Here you go." River handed me a funnel cake, wrapped in a napkin, and I took a hearty bite.

"Oh, my God, this is incredible!" I said around the mouthful of sweet dough practically melting on my tongue.

"Told you so," Doris said, accepting her own funnel cake.

"How much do we owe you?" Placing my dixie cup on the table, I reached into my shorts pocket for change.

"First one's on the house." River grinned. "Since this is your first Gravestone market and all."

I inclined my head. "Thank you, that's very generous."

With my belly full of iced tea and funnel cake, I realized River had been right. I felt better. Not cooler, but the sugar spike made the heat slightly more tolerable. Doris had been feeding Flynn tiny pieces of funnel cake, thinking I wouldn't notice, but the woman was as subtle as a sledgehammer. That and the crumbs bouncing off my collar bone and tumbling into my cleavage to stick uncomfortably amongst the sweat were perfect giveaways.

"I gotta get back to Bernadette," Doris said, dusting

off her hands. "There's a queue forming, and lord knows that woman doesn't work well under pressure."

"I'm going to take a look at Cody's *antiques*."

Doris grabbed my arm and looked me dead in the eye. "Don't you be messing with that man. He's trouble with a capital T. You're meant to be keeping a low profile, remember?"

"Oh, I remember all right. Don't worry, I'm just going to look. Plus, he's not there. His daughter is manning the booth. Perfect time for a little recon." I'd seen Cody heed his daughter's advice and head off while we'd been shoving funnel cake into our mouths.

"Holly." I heard the warning in Doris's voice. It was scary that I'd known her a few short days, yet she already knew me so well. Could be because we were both SIA—Doris retired, me in hiding. We were also both witches. And with Gravestone on a ley line that conveniently hid magic, I figured the SIA weren't the only ones using it to their advantage.

"Good morning. Sure is a hot one, eh?" The girl with the green hair beamed at me when I arrived at her booth. She was dressed in denim shorts and a white lace top, with not a bead of sweat in sight.

"It sure is," I agreed. "I'm new here. This is my first time at the market." Hoping to strike up a rapport with the girl, I plastered on a warm and sincere smile. At least, that's what I was going for. It may have turned into more of a grimace, but she smiled back, so I took it as a win.

"Welcome. I'm Macey. I come to the market every

month with my dad. We have an antique store in Corpus Christi, so we bring some of the smaller items to the market for a quick sale." From a distance, I'd thought Macey to be a teenager, but now, up close, I could see she was a little older, maybe early twenties.

"Hi, Macey, I'm Holly."

"So, Holly, see anything you like?" Macey waved her hand across the table between us, drawing my attention to the various antique looking items. There were a few occult bits and pieces, ceremonial daggers, candles and incense, a cauldron the size of my palm, a collection of crystal balls, a golden replica of the statue in the town square, plus a bundle of altar cloths.

I opened my mouth to say no when something caught my eye. "Actually..." I reached for a box buried beneath a stack of old books. "This looks interesting."

"It's a puzzle box," Macey said. "You have to solve a series of puzzles to open the box. People used to use them to hide their treasures or important documents."

"Kinda like a safe."

"Yeah, I guess you could say that."

The puzzle box was intricately made, with carvings etched into the wood. You could see the multiple joins where sections of the box opened or moved. The trick was to align the pieces of the box in the correct sequence to open it.

"How much?"

"A hundred."

"Dollars?" I laughed. "I don't think so. You don't

even know if this opens. What if it's damaged and is basically a decorative chunk of wood, nothing more?"

Her blue eyes widened, then narrowed. "Seventy-five."

"I'll give you twenty."

It was her turn to laugh. "Sorry, no can do. My dad would kill me if I let it go for less than fifty."

"Fifty it is." I had no idea if it was a fair price or not, but something about the box called to me. It practically vibrated in my hands. I had to have it.

"Sold."

We both grinned and while I paid, I said, "I saw your dad arguing with a couple just before. What was that about?"

She froze before quickly shoving my money into the cash tin she had under the table. "I don't know."

"The couple, the Whelans I believe, seemed mighty angry."

Her smile disappeared, and a shutter came down across her features, all pretense at friendliness gone. "Was there anything else I can help you with, Holly?" She put emphasis on my name, as if wanting me to know she remembered it.

I pursed my lips. "Nope. I think I got a bargain here today. I hope your dad doesn't get too mad at you for letting it go at such a cheap price."

Her face drained of all color, and I thought for a minute she was going to pass out. "What?" she squeaked.

"Relax, I'm just teasing." I felt like a bit of a heel and

quickly backtracked. "It's just a box, and it's going to look great on my dresser," I lied. I didn't have a dresser. I barely had furniture. I slept on a borrowed camp cot in my living room thanks to my cover story—that I'd arrived in Gravestone to claim my inheritance from my long-lost great uncle, John Smith. My inheritance? A run-down cottage, furniture that was only fit for the dump, and a ton of work.

Clutching the box to my chest, I bid Macey farewell and left to peruse the rest of the market. In the distance, the low rumble of thunder vibrated through the earth. Flynn, still on my shoulder, dug his claws in.

"I heard it," I assured him. "Pretty ominous, eh?"

I was admiring a blue crystal attached to a leather thong at a stall manned by two teenagers when a heavy hand clamped down on my shoulder, fingers digging in painfully. "Hey, you, there's been a mistake. That puzzle box isn't for sale!" Cody Pendant boomed in my ear.

Releasing the necklace, I ducked and spun, evading his hold, the box clamped to my chest, Flynn swinging from my hair at the sudden movement.

"Hands off," I growled, keeping my knees bent, body tense, ready to fight.

"Hand it over. That was never meant to be sold," he repeated, moving to snatch the box from me. I dodged and weaved, evading him.

"Too bad. Macey sold it to me. It's mine."

He lurched toward me, and I sidestepped, narrowly avoiding his outstretched hands. We danced around, him swearing and cursing as I evaded his attempts to wrestle the box from me. Until my walking boot let me down and I stumbled, landing on my rear, my teeth rattling at the impact.

Cody towered over me, blocking the light and looking generally menacing. A look he wore well. He bent, his beefy hands reaching for the box yet again when Flynn launched himself from my shoulder and flew through the air to land on Cody's hand, where he promptly sank his teeth into the man's flesh.

"Ow! What the hell?" Cody roared, shaking his hand to dislodge Flynn, who only clung on harder. That is, until Cody wrapped his other hand around Flynn's tiny body and squeezed.

"Hey!" I screeched from my position on the ground. "You're hurting him. Let him go, you bully!"

Cody paused in his squeezing and looked at me incredulously. "Bully?"

I shrugged. "Seems to fit. Flynn is a mere fraction of your size, and he was only protecting me. Let him go."

"This rodent is your… pet?" Cody couldn't have been more surprised if the sky had turned green.

I gave a curt nod. "Yes. Now release him."

"I'd do as the lady says," Sheriff Joshua Calder said from behind Cody. "Before she punches you in the face."

I leaned sideways to eyeball Calder, who was rubbing his jaw as if remembering the time I'd slugged him for shooting at Flynn. It had all been a terrible misunderstanding, but he'd wasted no time throwing me into a cell after the incident.

"Sheriff," I said in greeting, the puzzle box clutched to my chest. Calder stepped around Cody, offering a hand to haul me to my feet. I gladly accepted, placing my hand in his, heat rushing to my cheeks as a pulse of energy sparked where our palms touched. Calder gave me a look I couldn't interpret. Lust? Desire? Annoyance?

"What seems to be the problem here?" he asked.

Cody held Flynn up by the scruff of his neck, ignoring Calder and speaking directly to me. "I'll swap you. My puzzle box for the rat."

"I bought the puzzle box fair and square," I shot back, ignoring Flynn's outraged squeak as he dangled from Cody's grip.

"Give her the rat. Now," Calder growled, hand coming to rest on the holster at his hip. After a tense stand-off that lasted micro-seconds, Cody thrust Flynn toward me and let go. I caught him as he plummeted toward the ground, swinging him up and onto my shoulder where he assumed his usual position, one paw tightly gripping my hair, but I heard the frantic gasps of breath, knew Cody had hurt him, and my blood boiled. A shiver of magic danced across my knuckles before shooting up my arm. Feeling it, Flynn licked my neck.

"Ew. Gross," I hissed, knowing what he was doing. It was Flynn's job to remind me not to use my magic. Whenever he felt it powering through my body, he'd lick me as a not-so-subtle reminder... no magic. His lick was an effective deterrent—it grossed me out like you wouldn't believe.

"That," Cody pointed at the box still clutched to my chest, "is mine. I want it back."

I sucked in a calming breath, pushing my magic down. "I bought it for fifty bucks. From his booth. Ask Macey. She sold it to me. If he didn't want to sell it, he shouldn't have put it up for sale." I had no intention of handing it over. And okay, I admit, it was with a certain degree of childish petulance that I wanted to keep it purely because he wanted it. Which, of course, had me intrigued. What was so important about this box that Cody wanted it back so badly? You'd think he'd be grateful for a sale.

Calder ushered us back toward Cody's booth. "Let's find out, shall we?"

"Are you calling me a liar?" It was comical, really, since I'd been lying to everyone ever since I set foot in Gravestone.

"Did I say that?" Calder shot back, giving me an unfathomable look. A few short strides later and we were back at Cody's booth, Macey wringing her hands and looking guilty as sin.

"What did you do?" Cody snapped, face darkening by the second, a vein pulsing in his forehead.

"It was in a box under the table, and I thought you'd just forgotten to put it out, so… I put it out," she whispered, blue eyes huge in her pale face.

Cody slammed his fist down on the table, sending the whole thing shaking. A wooden candle holder toppled over. "You are useless!" He bellowed. "I don't know why I bother with you. You are a total waste of my time. Such a disappointment. I wish you were the son I wanted, not some useless *girl*."

My mouth dropped open, and my eyes were out on stalks. Before I could gather myself and come to Macey's defense, Cody swiveled on his heel and stalked away, Macey rushing after him. I couldn't make out what she was saying, but I caught the tone. Apologetic. Groveling.

I shot a glance at Calder, who gave me another one of his unfathomable looks and a shoulder shrug.

"See? Told you I didn't steal it."

His brows shot up. "Did I say you had?"

I opened my mouth to answer when it occurred to me that, no, he hadn't. No one had accused me of stealing the stupid puzzle box. Cody Pendant merely wanted it back. I cocked my head, wondering if I should sell it back to him for a tidy profit.

"I wouldn't if I were you," Calder drawled.

"Wouldn't what?"

"Whatever it is you're thinking of doing. I wouldn't. It can't be good."

As a Supernatural Investigation Agency agent, I was disconcerted that he already had me pegged. I was in Gravestone under cover, was meant to be keeping a lower than low profile and, above all else, stay off the local police's radar. Yet Sheriff Joshua Calder could read me like a book, and that not only rankled, it was concerning, for if he blew my cover, I'd have no option but to take him out. And I don't mean on a date.

I sniffed. "Whatever." *Snappy comeback*. I glanced up

at the sky, the clouds thicker, heavier, not so much gray as deep, dark purple with blue hues. They were incredibly beautiful but darkly ominous.

"Do you get a lot of storms?" I asked, remembering the rainstorm that had rolled in a few nights ago. Doris and I had taken advantage of the resulting power outage and broken into the mayor's home in hopes of finding evidence of her dabbling in witchcraft. Unfortunately, we'd come up empty-handed. Didn't mean the illustrious mayor was off my radar, though.

Calder tilted his head back, exposing the column of his throat, and I found myself strangely mesmerized.

"We get our fair share." He shrugged, eyes on the clouds overhead. A fork of lightning shot through the sky, followed by the rumble of thunder. "Don't think this is going to hold off for long, though."

"Will the market close early?" Such a shame. People had gone to a lot of effort.

Calder shook his head. "Nah, we'll batten down the hatches and wait for it to blow over. I checked the radar this morning. This squall should clear up by noon. You okay on your own? Time for me to get my deputy to start telling people to prepare for the storm."

Okay on my own? I almost choked on my own spit. "I'm sure I can manage." I did my very best not to roll my eyes, but I figured my face was doing something I wasn't aware of because he looked at me as if trying not to laugh before nodding and spinning on his heel to hurry away in search of his deputy.

Flynn yanked on my hair, his paw pointing. I

followed where he indicated. The path home. "You want to leave?" I asked, surprised he wanted to bail so early. He nodded his head vigorously.

"Tell you what—there's one booth that caught my eye that I want to visit, then we'll head home, okay?"

He sighed, as if to say *fine*. But it was a four-year-old's version of fine. A fine which meant it wasn't fine at all. Keeping a firm grip on the puzzle box, I hurried as much as I was able to a booth I'd spotted displaying brown hessian bags tied with string.

"Are these what I think they are?" I asked, picking up a bag, judging its weight. Had to be about five pounds.

"Flour. Yes." The short woman behind the table smiled and nodded. She had to be four feet, tops, and equally wide as she was tall. But her smile was warm, and the lines crinkling at the corners of her eyes told me she smiled a lot.

Putting the flour back on the table, I began reading the handwritten labels attached to each bag.

"Rye, oatmeal, buckwheat, whole wheat, cornmeal, rice. You have an impressive selection. Do you grow this yourself?"

"Some. Other times, I buy the grain and grind it into flour myself. These are all one hundred percent organic. Was there anything you wanted in particular?"

Thunder rumbled again, and we both glanced up. I knew as soon as the first drop of rain fell, she'd whip a tarp over her flour to protect it from the moisture. And if I wanted to spend the afternoon baking, which I did, then I needed to make my purchase quickly, before the rains came.

"I'll take a five-pound bag of rye and whole wheat, and a two-pound bag of pumpernickel, please."

She beamed, revealing a mouthful of crooked, yellow teeth. "Excellent choices. Now these cloth bags they're in, they're just for decoration, okay? The best way to store your flour when you get home is in an airtight container, yes?"

I smiled and nodded. "Yes. I know. Thank you."

"Do you *have* airtight containers?" she pressed, brown eyes shrewd. I chewed my lip and mentally went through my cupboards. I had airtight containers, yes, but most of them were in use storing the goodies I'd already baked. When I remained silent, she tsked and rummaged under the table, pulling out three huge glass jars with gold lids. "Here. You may buy these. You need to take good care of your flour. It's important."

"Okay."

"You are baking bread, yes?"

I blinked in surprise. I'd decided, when I'd seen her collection of flours, that I would indeed bake bread this afternoon, rather than the cakes, biscuits, and pies I usually baked. How did she know?

"I'm Cecilia. I know many things." She nodded, crossing her arms over her ample bosom. In her green floral dress with bright yellow apron, she looked as far from a psychic as you could get, but I couldn't help but wonder if she had the gift.

"How much do I owe you, Cecilia?"

"Two hundred dollars."

"What?" I wheezed, eyes practically watering at the exorbitant price tag.

"What?" she snapped. "You want store bought quality? You want plain old boring bread or you want excellent bread? You want bread that will melt on your tongue and fill your belly?" She kissed the tips of her fingers and rubbed her stomach in demonstration.

It was my turn to narrow my eyes and study her shrewdly. I was pretty sure she was playing me. I wouldn't be surprised if the flour in the bags was store bought and she'd simply decanted it into her cute handmade sacks and whacked on an outrageous mark up.

"How about you tell me the *real* price?" I suggested. "Because we both know that while flour is important, it's the baker that makes the bread, not the flour."

She sniffed and tossed her head in the air, but I caught her giving me the side eye, as if sizing me up. Seconds ticked by and another bright flash of lightning lit up the sky, quickly followed by a boom of thunder. The storm was closing in.

"Look," I finally said. "I'm not prepared to pay that much. I'll give you seventy. Including the glass jars."

"Eighty," she shot back.

"Deal." The truth was, I could have bought the flour cheaper elsewhere, but the general store didn't stock rye or pumpernickel. They'd have to order it in specially, which would take time.

"Pleasure doing business with you, Holly."

"How did you know my name?"

She tapped the side of her nose. "Best you hurry home. The rain is coming. I'm closing now. Shoo." She waved me away, shaking out a tarp to drape over her stall.

Picking up the string bag she'd provided that was full to overflowing with the flour and jars, I stepped back before she smacked me in the face with the tarp. Glancing around, I could see most stall holders were doing the same. Battening down and apparently settling in to wait for the storm to pass. I hobbled back to Doris's stall.

"You've been busy," she said, eyeing my purchases.

"Don't suppose you'd be able to give me a lift home?" I asked hopefully. "I wasn't expecting to buy three bags of flour, and they're heavy. Not to mention this puzzle box is a tad awkward."

"Where'd you get it? It's nice. I like it."

"Ha. Long story, but I got it from Cody Pendant's stall. His daughter sold it to me, only after I bought it, he told me it wasn't for sale and tried to make me give it back."

"Why bring it to the market if it's not for sale? Silly man." Doris shook her head. "Bernadette, I'm going to take a break and wait out the storm at Holly's house. You want to come with us?"

Bernadette, who'd been busily shoving her doilies into plastic bags, paused and glanced up. "Actually, yes. That would be lovely."

Doris rummaged in her purse and pulled out her

keys. "Here. Catch." She tossed them at me, but with my hands full, I had no chance of catching them, and they hit me in the chest before bouncing to the ground.

"You were supposed to catch them!" Doris shook her head at my apparent lack of reflexes.

I indicated the string bag with my flour purchases in one hand and the puzzle box in the other. "Hands are kinda full right now."

"Oh, yeah. So they are." Doris draped a plastic tablecloth over her stall, sat a rock on each corner to hold it down, then retrieved her keys. "Come on, Bernadette. Holly has the best snickerdoodle's you've ever tasted."

"Better than River's?" Bernadette finished securing her stall and joined us as we headed toward Doris's red Impala.

"Better than River's," Doris replied. "But don't tell River I said that."

CHAPTER
Three

The sound of creaking floorboards woke me. Sitting up, I swung my legs out of bed and paused to listen. There it was again. Overhead. I twisted, searching for Flynn in the little light filtering through the curtains, finally spotting him on the camp chair, sound asleep.

"Psst," I hissed, reaching over to poke him. He didn't stir, so I poked him again, harder. He was probably in a food coma, given the amount of bread he'd eaten throughout the day. After the storm had passed and Bernadette and Doris had returned to the market, I'd spent the afternoon baking bread, and it had been glorious. Slathering butter over thick slices of homemade bread and shoving it in our faces until our bellies were so full we could barely move had made for an early night.

Blinking his eyes open, Flynn stretched, his whiskers twitching. I put a finger to my lips and pointed to the ceiling. Flynn glanced up, his ears swiveling like radar dishes. Now he heard it. I pointed to the staircase, and he nodded. Fully alert, he nimbly leaped off the chair and scampered across the floor and up the stairs.

Wearing nothing but a tank top and panties, I followed, footsteps slow and silent, my walking boot laying on the floor by the bed. At the foot of the stairs, I paused to listen. It sounded like someone was in the master bedroom at the front of the house. The only thing in there was an old bookcase full to the brim with books. The second bedroom at the rear of the house held nothing but my suitcase, acting as a temporary wardrobe until I got something more permanent.

A breeze ruffled my hair, and I turned. I could just make out the back door standing open, moonlight filtering through the open doorway and casting shadows on the floor. I'd just taken a step toward it when an almighty bellow sounded from upstairs, followed by a crash that shook the entire house. A dark figure came barreling down the stairs, pushing past me and shoving me into the wall, Flynn in hot pursuit. Losing my balance, I staggered, trying not to put too much weight on my busted foot, while I peered after the intruder. Whoever it was had been dressed all in black, including a black hoodie, completely hiding their features. Pushing myself away from the wall, I hobbled to the back door and peered out. I couldn't see anything. No intruder and no Flynn.

Flicking on the kitchen light, I examined the back door, noticing the deep gouges in the wood where the lock had been jimmied. I was surprised the sound of that alone hadn't woken me. Instead, it had been their footsteps overhead. The question was, who was it and what were they looking for? Making my way upstairs, I examined the carnage in the master bedroom. The bookcase had toppled and shelves and books covered the floor. A dust plume hung in the air, and I sneezed, then sneezed again. Pressing my face into the crook of my elbow, I closed the bedroom door on the mess. Cleaning it up could definitely wait.

I was halfway down the stairs when Flynn returned, panting.

"Did you see where they went?" I asked, mindful of the twinge shooting up my leg, reminding me I was walking about without my walking boot.

Flynn shook his head, sides heaving.

"Did you at least catch a glimpse of their face? See who it was?"

He shook his head. I jerked my thumb, indicating the bedroom. "Was that you? Did you make the bookcase fall over?"

He blinked, his whiskers motionless before he glanced away and shrugged in a *maybe* gesture. I couldn't help but giggle. "It's okay," I reassured him. "I'm not mad." I figured Flynn must have startled the intruder, causing them to fall against the bookshelf, and the whole thing had toppled. All in all, a creative way to attempt to apprehend them.

His whole body relaxed, and I laughed out loud. Scooping him up, I settled him on my shoulder and made my way back into the living room. "There's no way I'm getting any more sleep tonight." Easing down on the cot, I strapped my foot into the walking boot while Flynn clung to my hair. His harsh panting slowly eased as he caught his breath.

Heading into the kitchen, I fired up the coffeepot before closing the back door. I tapped the lock. "I'll get a bolt for this tomorrow. I don't know what John Smith had been up to, but he must have something in this house that someone wants. What do you think it could be? A book of some sort, obviously—the intruder was searching the bookcase." My mind flicked back to a few nights ago, when Denise Hurt had dropped in, claiming John had promised to loan her a book. Then there was the mayor, who hadn't mentioned a book but had wanted to use my bathroom, which was conveniently located upstairs, next to the master bedroom with the now trashed bookshelf.

Flynn squeaked and shook his head.

"What? The intruder *wasn't* searching the bookcase?" Reaching for a cup from the hook suspended beneath an overhead cupboard, I set it down and waited for the coffee to finish brewing. Flynn squeaked and nodded.

"Wait. Is that a yes? He *wasn't* searching the bookcase? Or he *was* searching the bookcase?"

Flynn shook his head.

"Man, I wish you could talk. For one, you could tell me why your fur is purple." It had changed. Again. I had no idea why, or what—if anything—triggered it.

But it made taking him out in public a problem because people were bound to notice a purple rat. And that would lead to questions, and I was here to keep a low profile. Questions about me and my rat were best avoided.

"The question is, Flynn, who was our intruder? And how did they get past me? I didn't hear a thing until they were already upstairs. Which tells me whoever it was is a professional. If only my foot wasn't broken, I'd have been able to catch them, deal with it on the down-low."

Flynn squeaked and scratched, providing ever-so-helpful insight. With the coffee ready, I filled my cup, carried it to the kitchen table, and took a seat. Flynn leaped off my shoulder to the tabletop, grabbed the red and white checkered tea towel with his teeth, and tugged, revealing the puzzle box I'd bought at the market. We hadn't given it much attention since coming home, and it had gotten buried amongst the baking supplies, but now Flynn was reminding me it was here.

"What? You think our intruder was after this?"

Flynn shook his head.

"Oh, so what? You think three in the morning is a good time to see if we can get this thing open?"

He nodded, and I shrugged. "Well, why not? I'm too wired to sleep, and there's nothing I can do about securing that door until daylight. Let's see if we can't work out the puzzle and open the box."

I wish I could tell you that over the next few hours, when the sun streaked over the horizon and morning light bathed the kitchen, that we got the puzzle box open. We did not. I managed to move three pieces. Three! I was ready to hurl the thing into the wall. Or take it out into John Smith's garage and attack it with a hammer.

"Yoo-hoo!" Doris yelled a scant second before she began pounding on the front door. "Rise and shine!"

"I'm up, I'm up!" Throwing open the door, I leaned against the frame, forgetting I was in my underwear until she brushed past me with a wink and "nice outfit" comment.

"Coffee's on. Help yourself while I get dressed." After using the bathroom to freshen up, I pulled on a slightly wrinkled sundress, scooped my hair into a ponytail, and made my way back downstairs. "What brings you by so early?" I asked Doris. She was sitting at the kitchen table, half-finished cup of coffee in front of her, examining the puzzle box. Flynn watched with interest.

"It's hardly early. It's almost nine. Anyway, you were up."

"I've been up since three."

She paused in examining the box and looked at me, one brow raised. "Oh? Couldn't sleep?"

"We had an intruder." I told her about the break-in. I don't know what I'd been expecting—a little concern, a little outrage. Instead she said, "Cool," And went back to playing with the puzzle box. To my consternation, she managed to move a piece.

"You don't seem concerned." I pouted, slumping into the chair opposite her.

She shot me a hard look. "You prefer I run around in hysterics, clutching my pearls?"

"You're not wearing pearls."

She sniffed. "Not today. But I could go home and put them on just so I could clutch them."

"Not necessary." She was right. I didn't know what I was expecting. It wasn't like me to expect anything. I was an agent. A trained professional. Only my memory was like Swiss cheese—full of holes. Bits and pieces came back to me, but all in all, my mind was a mess, and I knew my reflexes weren't as sharp as they should be. It didn't help that I was sporting an injury. As each day passed, my fitness level sharply declined.

"So?" I prompted. "What brings you by? Not that it isn't lovely to see you," I tacked on.

"Church."

"Church?"

"Yes, and if we don't get a wriggle on, we'll be late."

I was already shaking my head. "Oh, no, I don't do church."

"You do in Gravestone." She put the puzzle box down, finished her coffee, and stood. "Let's go."

I remained seated. "I told you, I don't go to church. I'm not religious."

"Doesn't matter. Come on, get moving."

"Doris…"

"Holly." She sighed. "Your thinking is all wrong. You're here undercover. Hiding out, as you put it.

Instead, you need to think of it as an assignment. And your assignment is to blend. To fit in and not stand out —that's how you go unnoticed. And if you want to blend in in Gravestone, you get your butt into that church pew every Sunday morning."

She was right, and she knew it. I had to blend. I had to look like I belonged. And that meant going to church. I rubbed my temples as a headache started to pound behind my eyes. "Fine."

Piling into the passenger seat of her red Impala, I secured my seat belt, Flynn climbing from my shoulder onto the headrest. I'd been surprised he'd wanted to come with us. Maybe he was getting bored being left at home alone so much. "Better hold on tight," I told him. "She drives like a demon. And probably best to stay out of sight at church." The last thing I needed was the locals getting in hysterics at me, bringing my *pet* into a place of worship. As it was, the local mayor, Kerris Jones, had it in for Flynn, and if she spotted him, she'd have him *dealt with* before I could blink.

"After church, we'll go for lunch at River's," Doris said, peeling away from the curb with a squeal of tires.

Clutching the armrest, I nodded. "Sure."

Despite not being a church goer, I was actually grateful for Doris's friendship. I wasn't used to having friends. In the past, I'd had partners. Work colleagues. I knew they had my back, but that was different. They didn't actually care; they were just doing their jobs, as I was doing mine. None of them would turn up on my doorstep to take me to church on a Sunday morning.

Nor would they steal a boat and take me looking for human remains in the mangroves, shimmy up a tree to hide said human bones, or help me break into the mayor's house during a storm to try and find evidence that she was a murderer. *That's* what made Doris a friend.

We drove straight past the First Baptist Church, and I cleared my throat. "Um, isn't that the place?"

Doris shook her head. "We're going to St. Mary's."

"There's two churches in Gravestone?"

"There's three. But we don't talk about The Exalted Maple."

I briefly took my eyes off the road to stare at her, hard. "The Exalted Maple?" I'd never heard of such a religion—or church. Did they worship trees?

"Ever since High Priest Leonard had that *unfortunate* incident, well, they haven't had a Sunday sermon in a year. Most folks choose to worship at either St. Mary's or the First Baptist Church."

"What unfortunate incident?" I was dying to know what a priest could have gotten up to that led to the church not holding their usual Sunday worship, but Doris shook her head and said, "Shh, it's best not spoken of."

"Does it have anything to do with trees?"

"Oh, look, a seagull!"

"You know I'm not going to give up, so you may as well tell me," I pushed, for she had me intrigued.

"Okay fine. So, High Priest Leonard was conducting midnight mass, only we think he imbibed a little too much of the holy wine because instead of lighting incense, he lit a firecracker—heaven only knows how a firecracker got into the church in the first place. Perhaps one of the altar boys playing a prank? Anyway, the firecracker startled him, rightly so, only he panicked and tossed it into the congregation. No one was seriously injured, but a pew caught fire."

I smothered a laugh. "That doesn't seem serious enough to close the church for a year." Maybe if the church had burned down, but one pew? Hardly.

"Oh, it hasn't really closed. It's just High Priest Leonard took a sabbatical, and they haven't been able to get anyone to replace him."

"Right."

Turning onto Porter Road, I noticed a crowd gathering around the statue erected in the town center. Which wasn't really the town center, geographically speaking. The town square was a grass area with a yellow statue—I assumed they'd painted it to make it look gold, only the reality was, it looked like concrete painted yellow. The statue itself was of a woman with long, flowing hair cradling a seal. All very odd, but I was starting to appreciate the town of Gravestone was as quirky as the people who lived in it.

"Wonder what's happening?" Doris muttered, slowing to a crawl, neck craned as she tried to get a look.

"This isn't usual? You don't all meet before church?" St. Mary's was conveniently located next door to the town square. I'd figured the people milling about were just shooting the breeze before heading into the church.

"Nope." We parked the Impala and piled out.

"Stay out of trouble," I said to Flynn after we'd crossed the road. Setting him down on the grass, I watched as he immediately headed toward the statue.

Doris was two steps ahead, pushing her way through until she was at the front of the crowd. "Well, I'll be damned."

Now my interest was piqued, and I limped a little faster to join her.

"Okay, everyone, back up, back up." Calder approached from the other direction, yelling to make himself heard over the shocked gasps and whispers. For there, on the ground at the base of the statue, lay Cody Pendant. Dead.

Four

Standing slightly behind Doris, I peered over her shoulder. Cody was face down, his head turned to the side, blood covering the back of his head. He was in the jeans and button down he'd been wearing the day before.

"Not my intruder, then," I murmured to myself.

"Did you think he was?" Doris whispered back.

"It had crossed my mind." But the intruder had been dressed in black from head to toe and, now that I looked at Cody, the intruder had been smaller too. "It wasn't him."

"Ladies." Our whispering caught Calder's attention, and he moved toward us. "Can you back it up a step? Or ten." He approached with arms spread wide in an attempt to herd everyone back. "Preferably off the grass. This whole area is a crime scene."

More and more people arrived for church, saw the commotion, and wandered over to see what the fuss was about. Flynn had scampered up the statue and was now tucked in against the woman's neck, unnoticed. But he had a bird's-eye view of the crime scene. I saw him look my way and give a nod, so I gave him the thumbs up, hoping he'd spot some good intel he could pass on later. I refused to dwell on the fact that communication between us was difficult. We'd managed thus far—we'd find a way.

Deputy Laura Biden arrived, looking flustered. Guess she hadn't been expecting a murder this morning. Calder drew her attention to her misbuttoned shirt and stood sentinel while she turned her back and fixed her uniform. While Calder began to search Cody's body, Laura herded us away, but as soon as she turned her back, the crowd crept forward again.

"He's got something in his hand," Calder said. Snapping on a pair of gloves, he unfurled Cody's fingers. In his palm, a piece of paper.

"What is it?" whispered among the crowd.

"It's a note," Laura replied, then clamped her mouth shut tight when Calder shot her an annoyed glare. Her cheeks blushed bright red.

We watched in silence as Calder unfurled the scrap of paper, and he and Laura read it, then looked at me. Before I could gather a coherent thought, Laura was charging across the ground, one hand at her belt, whipping out her handcuffs.

"Holly Day! You're under arrest for the murder of Cody Pendent," she yelled.

The crowd scattered as if I'd dropped a lethal fart. Except for Doris, who remained steadfast by my side.

"What?" I blinked in shock. "I didn't kill him. Why would I? And what evidence do you have that says I did?"

But Laura kept coming, tackling me to the ground and rolling me onto my stomach. She was stronger than she appeared. With my face smashed into the grass I could just make out the gasps of the crowd and Doris's outraged, "Hey!" before my arms were yanked behind my back, practically dislocating my shoulders, and the steel of the cuffs slapped around my wrists. I was stunned she'd managed to get the jump on me. Since when had I become so sloppy?

"On your feet," Laura snarled, nudging me with her foot.

"Bit hard with my hands behind my back." I spat out a blade of grass.

"Deputy." There was a warning in Calder's tone, but Laura ignored it and him, hauling me to my feet, puffing and straining, as if I weighed a ton. I was marched none-too-gently to the police cruiser parked at the curb and bundled into the back seat. I looked out the window at Doris, her expression no doubt matching mine. Flabbergasted. How on Earth had I managed to get myself arrested for murder on my way to church?

While all eyes were on me, Flynn climbed down the statue and sniffed around Cody's body before streaking across the ground, his purple fur a blur. Next thing I knew, he'd leaped through the deputy's open driver's side window, shimmied under her seat, and popped up next to me in the back. I couldn't help but laugh. "Oh, hey."

Laura slid behind the wheel, gunned the engine, and shot off, flinging me backward. Doing my best not to topple over, I caught sight of Calder's face as we tore past. He wore a mixture of incredulity and resignation, and just before we careened around the corner, he ran his hand around the back of his neck and shook his head while Doris moved in on him.

"I guess this is one way of getting out of church," I said to Flynn.

"What was that?" Laura asked, eyes locking on me through the rearview mirror.

"Nothing. So, what makes you think I killed him?" I asked conversationally.

"He had your name and address on that note in his hand."

My eyes narrowed, digesting that piece of information. "Curious," I said. "And that makes me guilty how?" She didn't answer, but I knew she was thinking hard. I could practically hear the cogs grinding. "Think about it," I prompted. "If I'd killed him, wouldn't I have removed any incriminating evidence? Not that the note is incriminating evidence, FYI. It's a note. A piece of paper with writing on it. Just because my name is on that piece of paper does not mean I killed him."

"Shut up," she growled, pulling up with a jerk outside the police station. I wasn't processed. I was marched straight out the back to the cells. Flynn followed, keeping out of sight. As soon as Laura removed my cuffs and slammed the cell door shut, storming off in a bizarre fit of temper, Flynn squeezed through the bars and joined me on the cot.

"This has been the weirdest morning ever," I said. He lay down and began grooming himself. "By all means. Take a bath."

Laying on the cot, I stared at the ceiling, watching the metal blades of the overhead fan lazily spin. This wasn't the first time I'd been in Gravestone's lockup, and I was starting to think it wouldn't be my last. The law enforcement here liked to lock you up first, ask questions later.

"So, couple of questions." I was talking to myself but also to Flynn. "First of all, what was Cody doing with my name and address? He wasn't my intruder. Too big. And he's wearing the same clothes he was wearing yesterday. Our intruder wore black. You wouldn't get changed, break in, then get changed back into your old clothes again. Would you?"

Flynn squeaked.

"I mean, I guess it's possible. But anyway, the build is all wrong. It wasn't him. Maybe he paid someone to break in and steal the puzzle box?"

Flynn made a chittering noise in response.

"I agree." I craned my neck to look at him. "It's plausible. So, the second question is, who killed him? You and I both know it wasn't me. We already know he wasn't a popular man. There was that couple from yesterday he was arguing with. What were their names?"

No response from Flynn, and a quick glance revealed him splayed on his back with his paws spread eagle, fast asleep.

"Fat lot of help you are." Then it hit me. "Beau and Claire Whelan. The newlyweds. Cody ripped them off with a fake antique. Were they angry enough to kill him?"

Flynn snored.

"And what about his daughter, Macey? He was really nasty to her. Did she snap and bash his head in?" I sat up. "Wait a minute. I didn't see a murder weapon at the scene. Did you?" To the untrained eye, Cody's injuries were self-evident. A blow to the head. If I could examine the wound, I could determine what sort of weapon we were looking for. An object with a round edge, like a baseball bat? Or something with a sharp, straight edge? Or was his wound jagged, inflicted with a rock? All good questions and ones I couldn't answer without examining the victim for myself.

Another snore. Before I could poke Flynn and wake him up, I heard footsteps approaching. Swinging my legs over the edge of the cot, I rearranged the skirt of my dress to hide the rat.

Calder approached, the keys to the cell dangling from his fingers. Without a word, he unlocked the cell door and stood back, holding the door open wide in an invitation to leave.

"I take it I'm free to go?" I drawled, standing,

completely forgetting that I was meant to be hiding Flynn.

"You are." His jaw was tight, and if I didn't know better, I'd say he was grinding his teeth.

I smiled widely, enjoying his discomfort. "An apology would be nice. Because I'm pretty sure this," I waved my hand around the cell, "constitutes a wrongful arrest. Maybe even harassment."

"Holly Day, on behalf of the Gravestone Police Department, I offer our sincere apology for the situation that unfolded this morning and your subsequent wrongful arrest."

Despite asking for an apology, I hadn't been expecting one. I peered closely at Calder. "Everything okay? You're not sick, are you?"

"If you call a public interrogation by Doris Shutt as to why my deputy had just arrested you feeling sick? Then yes. I'm feeling very sick."

"Oh."

"Doris is out front. Please don't keep her waiting."

CHAPTER

Five

Not needing to be told twice, I hurried out of the cell, the clunk of my walking boot loud in the silence of words unspoken that hung in the air.

"Holly?" Calder called after me.

I turned. "Yes?"

"Take your rat with you."

"Right." Hurrying back, I scooped up the still snoozing Flynn, cradled him against my stomach with one hand, and brushed past Calder, who sucked in a breath at the contact.

"Don't worry, he doesn't have rabies," I snapped, bristling yet again at Calder's hostility toward Flynn. If he replied, I didn't hear it, deciding it was in my best interests to vacate the premises as quickly as possible before some other trumped-up reason found me back in the cells.

"You missed church." Doris was leaning against the hood of her Impala, arms crossed.

"Believe me, it wasn't intentional. Why did it take Calder so long to release me?" It had to be close to two hours since the deputy had thrown me in the slammer.

"Apparently," the way Doris dragged out the word told me she didn't entirely believe what she was about to say, "he couldn't leave the crime scene unattended. I said it wasn't, there were dozens of people there, but he says we didn't count. It had to be law enforcement, and his only deputy had just left."

I felt it was only fair to point out that he had a point. "He has a point."

"She should never have arrested you."

"Now that, we can agree on. Come on, let's go get lunch. Who do you think killed Cody Pendant?"

"The list is long. Pretty much every resident of Gravestone has had a run-in with the man at one time or another. Could be anyone."

At River's, the café was abuzz with talk of Cody's murder and my subsequent arrest.

"If it isn't the jail bird herself," River greeted us with a smile and a wink. "Out on bail?"

"Har har," I fake laughed. "I'm sure *you* know the whole thing was a colossal misunderstanding and that I'm *not* guilty of anything… but this lot? I'm not so sure." The locals who were occupying half the tables in River's café were now watching us, no doubt straining to hear what was being said.

"Ignore them." River waved a hand in dismissal. Handing us both a menu, she said, "Take a seat anywhere. I'll be by to take your order shortly." She took one step away, paused, and pivoted. "Actually, I may have a lead for you."

"A lead?" I shot a look at Doris, then back at River. "*We're* not investigating this."

"Says you," Doris huffed, crossing her arms over her chest.

"Do you want to hear or not?"

Of course we did. Knowing I was beat, I nodded. River indicated we should move in close, so we wouldn't be overheard. "Yesterday afternoon, at the market after the storm had passed, I saw Dino Cittadino threaten Cody," she whispered.

"Threaten how?"

"Knife to the throat type threaten." River looked over her shoulder, a frown creasing her brow. "He said something to him, but I couldn't make it out. But I got the overall tone. Menacing."

My eyes bugged out on stalks. This Dino character had held a knife to Cody's throat, and I was the one to get thrown in jail? "You've got to tell Calder," I said.

But River was shaking her head. "No way. I'm not getting involved. Plenty of other people witnessed it. I'm not risking my business. The last thing I need is to be firebombed."

"Firebombed? Why on earth would you be firebombed?"

"Doris, explain it to her, would you? I'll be back to take your order in a second." She hurried away while Doris grabbed my arm and dragged me to our usual table.

"Well?" I hissed. "What the hell was that about? Who is this Dino guy?"

"Dino Cittadino works for the Tarkath Syndicate. He comes to the Gravestone market now and then."

I flopped back in my chair, mouth open. The Tarkath Syndicate were thugs. Mobsters of magic. River was right. You didn't want to mess with them. I didn't blame her for not wanting to get involved.

"I see you've heard of them," Doris said, looking at me over the top of her menu.

I snorted. "Who hasn't? I've often wondered if they're behind the wand smuggling ring that landed me here."

"Sounds like something they'd do, for sure," Doris agreed. "I think I might try something new today." She laid the menu on the table and pointed. "I'm thinking the apple smoked bacon with a scoop of breakfast spuds."

"Yeah, yeah, sounds good." I was too distracted by this latest piece of information to worry about what to order. With a member of the Tarkath Syndicate in town, was my cover about to be blown? And why now? Had word leaked that I was here, and that's why this Dino guy was around? Was he searching for me? I shifted uncomfortably in my seat. I could practically feel the crosshairs on my back. And what was the altercation with Cody about? Was he pumping him for information about me?

I was considering asking for my food to go when the door opened, and Macey Pendant stepped inside with a man I'd never seen before. He had one hand on her shoulder in a comforting gesture. As per usual, every head turned to check out the newcomers.

"Who's that with Macey?" I asked Doris, watching as the couple made their way to a table. I pegged the guy to be mid-forties, six foot two, a hundred and eighty-five pounds, give or take. The way he moved, with a hidden stealth, warned me there was more to him than what met the eye. Was he with the Tarkath Syndicate, too?

Doris swiveled to look. "Dunno. Never seen him before. He's a bit of alright, though."

I continued studying the man, agreeing with Doris's assessment. Besides being easy on the eye, I didn't miss the way he chose the seat that kept his back to the wall or the way his eyes clocked the exits, all the while paying close attention to Macey. This guy was a professional. Another shiver shot up my spine, and I was contemplating bolting when River returned.

"So, what'll it be, ladies?"

"Eggs and pancakes with two bacon and a caramel latte," Doris declared.

I glanced at her over my menu. "I thought you were having apple smoked bacon with a scoop of breakfast spuds."

"Doris is a creature of habit," River told me. "Despite a genuine interest in trying other items on the menu, she always orders the same thing."

"Right. Well, if she's having the pancakes—again— then I'll try the apple smoked bacon with a scoop of breakfast spuds. And no, you can't have any," I added for Doris's benefit, not missing how her eyes lit up when she heard my order. "Black coffee."

"Won't be long." River moved away, and as she did so, the man who'd come in with Macey stepped forward. He'd been standing behind her, and I hadn't seen nor heard him approach. His sudden appearance startled me, and I sucked in a breath on a gasp.

"Sorry." He smiled, his eyes twinkling. "Didn't mean to scare you."

With my heart thundering in my chest so hard the pulse in my neck had to be clearly visible, I offered a weak smile. "You didn't."

He smirked but didn't call me out on the lie. "Sorry to interrupt, but my friend, Macey," he jerked his thumb toward the table where Macey was sitting, watching, "told me you were the one who bought the puzzle box from her dad yesterday."

My eyes narrowed. The box again. Had *he* been the one who'd broken into my house?

"What of it?"

"The thing is, Cody acquired the puzzle box for me. It was never meant to be sold. That was an honest mistake by Macey. Her dad hadn't told her the piece was on commission."

"And you are?" Doris interrupted.

The man smiled, flashing straight white teeth. "Where are my manners? I'm Keelan Moore." He reached for Doris's hand and brought the back of it to his lips, bestowing her with a kiss.

"Doris Shutt," she breathed, batting her eyelashes.

His smile deepened. "A pleasure to meet you, Doris. And you are?" He turned that dazzling smile to me, and I felt a pulse of magic blast me in the face, jerking my head back. But the magic wasn't… unpleasant. It was kinda warm and soothing. He was using a charm.

Narrowing my eyes, I held out my hand and shook his, my grip firmer than it needed to be. "Holly Day."

"A pleasure, Holly. Look, I'm sorry about the mix-up. It's all been a terrible misunderstanding. The truth is, I'd already paid a deposit for Cody to acquire the puzzle box on my behalf. I'm here to pay the balance and collect the box."

"Is that right?" He'd kept a hold of my hand, and I felt him pushing his magic into me, felt it traveling up my arm, its tingling presence making the hairs stand on end. I snatched my hand away, breaking the connection. His dark eyes flared with annoyance, his composure slipping, revealing his true nature for a split second before he regained control. But in that split second, I saw him. The true him. Dark and rotten to the core. The charming smile and twinkling eyes were nothing more than a mask.

"I'm sure we can come to some sort of arrangement," Doris said, clearly under his thrall. "Isn't that right, Holly?"

"Actually, no. That's not right." I doubled down on refusing to part with the puzzle box. Call me stubborn. Or stupid. But there was something about the box that had me intrigued, and I was determined to find out what it was. Its appeal only increased because Cody, and now Keelan, wanted it so badly.

Seeing that I was resisting his magic, Keelan deftly pulled out a chair and took a seat, his knee bumping mine beneath the table. "Holly, I'm here to make a deal. Tell me what it is you want in exchange for the puzzle box, and I'll make it happen. Money? Not a problem. Name your price. Something else? You'll find I'm a well-connected, resourceful man. Tell me… what will it take?" He placed his hand over mine on top of the table, and when I went to jerk away, he pressed down hard, trapping my hand beneath his.

"I suspect you've already tried to liberate the puzzle box from my possession," I hissed. "And don't think I don't know what you're doing, using some sort of spell to make me do what you want. You should know that won't work with me, so don't waste your time."

He cocked his head, his mouth opening to reply, but whatever he'd been about to say was lost in a chorus of screams and yells as a commotion broke out behind us.

"Rat! There's a rat!"

Chaos erupted. Patrons leaped to their feet and chairs toppled. The charm Keelan had been using fell away to be replaced by red hot rage. It burned through him and into me, the searing pain where our skin touched immediate. Snatching my hand away, I surged to my feet, clutching my hand to my chest, where the skin continued to throb. I daren't look. I daren't take my eyes from Keelan. Something told me he was a very dangerous man, despite his charming exterior.

Between one blink and the next, he regained control. The anger disappeared as quickly as it had arrived and back in its place, the charming man. He inclined his head, stood, and without a word, returned to Macey, who was on her feet, her eyes scanning the floor for the rat everyone was in hysterics about.

Oh my God, a rat. It had to be Flynn. Scanning the room, I caught sight of a flash of purple fur scampering across the floor, deftly avoiding stamping feet and crashing chairs.

"Flynn!" I yelled, stepping away from the table and bending, hand outstretched, ready to scoop up my wayward rat before someone landed a blow. Seconds later, I was holding him to my chest, his heart pounding in time with mine.

"Sorry, folks," I apologized to the room in general. "This is Flynn. He's my pet, and I know he's a rat, but please don't panic. He won't hurt you. And he's perfectly clean." I was met with muttering, comments about vermin, and general disbelief.

"Holly." River was frowning, drying her hands on a dish cloth as she approached. "We can't have animals inside the café. Pet or not."

I nodded. "No, I know. Sorry. He was asleep in Doris's car. He must've woken up and come looking for me. We'll leave—can we get our order to go? I'll wait outside for it."

"Fine." She gave a curt nod and led the way to the side door, holding it open for us to pass through.

"Sorry," I said as I brushed past her.

"Look, I don't have a problem with you having a pet rat. Quite frankly, you can have whatever kind of pet you want. I couldn't care less. But what I do care about is you bringing a rat into my café. That's the sort of thing that can get me shut down. If Kerris hears about this, there will be hell to pay."

Kerris Jones was Gravestone's mayor, and she already hated Flynn. If she caught so much as a whisper that Flynn had been in River's café, she'd have the café shut down before you could blink.

"I'm sorry. Look, if she does hear about it, I'll explain what happened." Not that I held out any hope that Kerris would listen.

"It's a health code violation."

"I know. I'm sorry." I didn't know what else to say. I hadn't been expecting Flynn to come looking for me. To others, he was nothing more than a rat, but I knew the truth. He was a man, trapped in a rat's body. More than a man, he was a shifter. Despite taking on some definite rat characteristics, he still had the mental capacity of a man. He wouldn't have come into the café unless he needed to. Had he felt Keelan's magic and came to warn me?

"I'll bring your meals out." She shut the door, and I watched through the glass as she stalked away, back ramrod straight. I turned to Doris, who was being uncharacteristically silent.

"Everything okay?" I asked. "You don't mind not eating here, do you?" I didn't want to upset River more than she already was. Not to mention it was a thousand degrees outside, and despite the outdoor tables having umbrellas, the heat was relentless. The idea of eating at one of the outdoor settings was less than appealing.

"It's hot out here. I think I'll wait inside."

"Doris?" I grabbed her arm to stop her from leaving. "Is everything okay? Are you mad at me? About Flynn?" Flynn was now in his usual spot on my shoulder.

"You've opened this can of worms. Now, lie in it." She opened the door and stepped back into the café, leaving me standing outside.

"What did *that* mean?" Flynn chittered something I couldn't understand in response. "Today has been all sorts of crazy, and it's only lunchtime." Sighing, I headed down the narrow, paved path that skirted the outside of River's café, my boot making its familiar thunk. I talked to Flynn as I walked. "Why did you come inside?"

Flynn squeaked and ran down my arm, claws gripping into my skin. "Ow!" I protested, lifting my arm. Then I saw what he was pointing at. The burn on the back of my hand. I slowed, examining the mark. "Did you feel his magic? Is that what brought you inside?"

Flynn nodded, then began speaking in animated squeaks, standing on his hind legs, front legs waving in the air, ending with him pointing at the café.

"Trouble is, Flynn," I responded. "I have no idea what you just said."

He slumped in defeat.

"Hey," I chided. "We can work this out. The man who did this, his name is Keelan Moore, and he was definitely using magic. He had Doris under his thrall, but it didn't work with me. He said that Cody had procured the puzzle box for him. He was after a deal for me to sell it to him."

Flynn waved a paw as if to say, *continue.*

"He came in with Macey. Which I guess gives some validity to his story. They appear to know each other. So, Cody gets his hands on the puzzle box, arranges to meet Keelan at the market to complete the transaction and hand it over. Only Macey, not knowing about their arrangement, puts it out on the table to sell. And I buy it.

"When Cody finds out she's sold it, he freaks and tries to buy it back from me. You know," I rubbed my chin, deep in thought, "if he'd asked nicely, I totally would have. But I'd seen the way he'd treated the Whelans. The man was a brute and a bully. Plus, I'm totally intrigued about why Cody wanted it back so badly. I don't even think the puzzle box is worth that much, so I'm thinking it's not the box itself. It's what's inside. And *that's* what Keelan Moore is here for."

CHAPTER

Six

"I feel hungover," Doris admitted, sitting opposite me at my kitchen table, empty takeout containers from River's all that were left of our lunch.

"I'm not surprised. Keelan Moore was using magic. You were under some sort of charm spell."

"I was? The nerve of that man!"

"I think that's why Flynn came bursting into the café. He sensed the magic."

"River was pretty mad, huh?"

"You were too. You said that I'd opened a can of worms and that I had to lie in it."

"What can of worms?"

"My thoughts exactly." Leaning back in my seat, I gazed up at the ceiling. "Keelan Moore and his use of magic aside, we now have three suspects in Cody Pendant's murder. Beau and Claire Whelan," I ticked off on my fingers. "Dino Cittadino. And Keelan Moore."

"Keelan's a suspect?"

"You sound surprised." I got up to pour another cup of coffee. "Keelan hired Cody to acquire the puzzle box. The one that I bought from their stall."

"Oh. So you think when Cody told Keelan he'd sold it to someone else, Keelan got mad and killed him?"

"It's a possibility. I think there's something inside the puzzle box, and that is what this is all about."

"Something worth killing over." Doris nodded.

"Agreed. We need to get the box open."

Clearing away the takeout containers, I retrieved the puzzle box from where I'd hidden it in the cupboard under the sink. Not the safest of places, but I'd already decided if we couldn't get it open, I'd send Doris up the cedar elm tree in the back yard to tape the darn thing to a branch for safe keeping. It had worked for Seth Saltzman's bones.

Resuming my seat, I studied the box, turning it this way and that, randomly pressing, trying to see if any hidden compartment moved, or even better, popped open. Doris watched for a while, then demanded I hand it over.

"You think you can get it open? Be my guest." Handing her the box, I gulped down the remainder of my coffee and stood. "I'm going to freshen up. How long do we give this before we take that thing out to the shed and bust it open with John's tools?" John Smith had been a carpenter. I was confident I'd find something in his shed that would get the job done.

"How long is a piece of cake?" Doris replied, tongue

poking out as she repeated the exact same actions I'd taken.

Chuckling to myself, I headed upstairs, Flynn bounding behind me.

"Wait out here," I instructed. "I need to pee. Then you can play under the faucet."

I thought I heard him sigh as he veered off and headed toward the front bedroom but couldn't be sure. With a shrug, I stepped into the bathroom, shoved the door in a fruitless attempt to get it closed. Given its warped state, I knew it wouldn't, but still, I tried. I don't know what I was expecting, that one day it would magically decide it would no longer be warped and you could close it? But this house wasn't magic—the dilapidated appearance was testament to that, and the only way this door would close was if I repaired or replaced it. Which reminded me, I needed to follow up with Matt Casey, Gravestone's handyman and carpenter, and see where he was with the quote I'd requested.

Sitting on the toilet, I examined the back of my hand where Keelan's touch had burned me, running my fingers softly over the tender skin. The rune on my collarbone tingled, then stung like I'd been zapped with static electricity.

"Ouch," I hissed, snatching my fingers away, then holding my hand in front of my face in disbelief. The burn mark was gone! Hurrying to the washbasin, I examined my reflection in the cracked mirror above it, pulling the strap of my dress aside to check on the rune shaped birthmark, only to gasp in shock. It was darker. Not bigger, just darker. Like the rune had healed the burn inflicted by Keelan and absorbed it. Which made sense. Doris had told me the rune wasn't a birthmark at all but a protection spell put upon me. She'd called it an Algiz rune, meaning defense and protection.

Only I didn't remember any of it. Who had marked me with the rune, and why? All I knew was that I was protected.

Flynn, having heard the toilet flush, squeezed through the gap in the door, climbed the shower curtain, and jumped onto the edge of the basin. Turning on the faucet, I washed my hands, then left the tap running for Flynn, who loved to play and bathe beneath the water's flow.

"Holly!" Doris yelled from downstairs.

"Did you get it open?" I yelled back, turning off the faucet despite Flynn's protests and hurrying back downstairs. I appeared in the kitchen doorway, expecting to find the puzzle box open. It wasn't.

"What? No." Doris scoffed. She held up her phone. "Vera says Beau and Claire Whelan just walked into the police station."

"Under arrest?"

Doris shrugged. "Dunno. But if that were the case, Vera would probably have said they'd just been arrested. So, I'm assuming they're *helping the sheriff with his investigation*." She air quoted. Tossing her phone back into her purse, she swung it over her shoulder. "Come on."

I grabbed the puzzle box off the table. "Where are we going?"

"To do a little snooping." She eyed the puzzle box clutched to my chest. "You're bringing it?"

I nodded. "Someone broke in last night. Initially, it didn't click that they may have been looking for this. It was buried beneath a dish towel on the table, so whoever was looking didn't look very hard. But whatever, that doesn't matter. What matters is that Keelan Moore wants it. He may have been behind the break-in. Until I get this open, it's not leaving my sight."

"Right. Come on then."

"Are you sure you've never seen him before?" I quizzed, following her out of the house. "Flynn, you'd better stay here, keep an eye on things, okay?"

He gave me a thumbs up.

"Not that I recall, but *if* he's been using magic like you say, then maybe I have seen him around and just don't remember," Doris said.

"You don't believe me? Why would I lie about him using magic?"

"I'm not saying you lied. I'm saying I don't remember."

"Well, take my word for it. He was. And I can't help but wonder if Macey Pendant is under his spell."

"Could well be," Doris admitted. I climbed into the passenger seat of the Impala, the heat from the seat searing the back of my thighs. Doris fired up the car and pulled away from the curb with her customary spinning of wheels, gravel spraying as she fishtailed down Berryman Street while I clutched the door handle and battled the impulse to squeeze my eyes shut. I was an SIA agent. Brave. Fearless. Except when it came to little old ladies driving cars they could barely see over the steering wheel, like she was qualifying for NASCAR.

"I know you said we were snooping, but where, exactly, are we going?"

"The Whelans' farmhouse. Vera said they just walked into the police station, we assume to give a statement about the altercation they had with Cody yesterday. So, we know they're not home."

"You know where they live?"

"Of course! Relax, it's a ten-minute drive, tops."

"There was no sign of a murder weapon at the town center, but the amount of blood at the scene tells me Cody was killed there."

"Agreed." Doris nodded, then put on her indicator for a nano-second before yanking on the wheel and turning onto a side street. My head hit the side window.

"Geez, take it easy, would you?" I grumbled, rubbing my head. "So, anyway, nothing at the scene that could have been used to bash Cody over the head. Meaning the killer took it with him. Or her."

"Yeah, but you'd ditch it at the first opportunity, wouldn't you?"

"If it was a rock or something like that, absolutely. I'd probably walk down the pier and throw it in the ocean." I dusted my hands. "So, the likelihood of us finding the murder weapon at the Whelans' is pretty slim."

"Assuming Cody was whacked over the head with a rock," Doris said.

"Assuming that," I agreed. We needed to find out what Cody's autopsy revealed. Had a rock killed him? Or some other object, like a bat? Or a hammer? Because if it was an everyday item, the killer might not have ditched it. They may have cleaned it and put it back where it belonged. "You know Beau and Claire Whelan. Do you think they're capable of murder?"

"Anyone is capable of murder," Doris shot back.

"Sadly, you're not wrong." We lapsed into silence for the rest of the ride, each lost in our own thoughts. Ten minutes later, almost to the minute, Doris turned off the main highway and onto a dirt track. She slowed as we rolled past a wooden sign hanging by chains off a tree branch that read *Whelan*.

"Told you I knew where it was."

"I'm so pleased," I teased. "We have to be fast. There's only one road in and out. We don't want to get caught."

"Relax, it'll be fine."

"The more you tell me to relax, the more un-relaxed I become."

"I noticed."

The dirt track was bumpy, and Doris slowed to a crawl, which was amazing in itself. Eventually, we reached the farmhouse, pulling to a stop beside a red barn, engine idling.

"Maybe park around the back," I suggested. "Where we can't be seen if someone approaches."

"Roger that." Doris eased her foot off the brake, and the car crawled forward. She tucked it in close to the back of the barn, out of the direct line of sight should anyone come up the mile-long driveway. Of course, if the Whelans did come home, our cover would be well and truly blown, but at least we'd have a few scant minutes to return to the car and hopefully make a getaway without getting caught.

Leaving the puzzle box in the footwell, I opened the door and climbed out. Despite the sun blazing overhead, a chill settled over me, and I rubbed my arms.

"Do you feel that?" I asked Doris.

Slamming the car door so hard the whole car shook, Doris nodded. "Sure do. An enchantment?"

"It feels…"

"… sinister," she finished.

"Are Beau and Claire paranormal?"

"Dunno. But how cute is their farmhouse?" I turned to follow Doris's gaze. She was right. The farmhouse was the epitome of cute. The weatherboard was painted in a charming shade of sky blue, with white trim and shutters. A matching white picket fence bordered the small front garden, separating the house from the rest of the farm.

"Pretty darn cute," I had to agree. "What do they do? For a living."

"Beau is a farm hand, and Claire is a primary school teacher."

"Hardly criminal masterminds, then."

"Maybe. Maybe not."

"Okay, look, we don't have much time, and considering we don't even know what we're looking for —" I began, but Doris cut me off.

"Anything incriminating."

"Which," I pointed out, "could be anything. Let's split up. Why don't you take the barn, and I'll take the house?"

"Okay, I'll do the house. You do the barn."

I snorted out a half laugh. "Fine. But keep an eye on the time. Twenty minutes, Doris. Tops. Then we meet at the car, got it? And for the love of coffee, if you hear a car approaching, get back to the Impala immediately."

"Roger that."

I watched Doris re-enact Mission Impossible as she made her way to the house, crouching, ducking, and rolling, hands clasped together, fingers pointing like a fake gun. She stealthily—and I use that term loosely—climbed the three steps to the front porch, then flung herself against the weatherboard siding, back pressed to the wall. Keeping herself pressed against the wall, she crept along until she reached the side of the house, then disappeared from view.

With far fewer theatrics, I made my way to the barn. Opening the door, I slipped inside, taking a moment for my eyes to adjust to the dim light. Dust mites danced in the air, and looking at the junk strewn around, I figured it was a fair assessment that the barn hadn't been used in a long time.

I gave it a cursory inspection, but considering the heavy coating of dust and cobwebs on the tools hanging on the wall, none of them had been used to belt Cody over the back of the head. Letting myself out of the barn, I headed to the house, keeping one eye on the driveway in case the Whelans return.

"Doris?" I stage-whispered, easing through the open back door.

"In here," she called. I followed the sound of her voice. The back door opened directly into the kitchen, which was separated from the living room with a half wall. Leading off the living room was a bedroom, and that's where I found Doris, examining a round rug placed between a dresser and the wrought iron bed.

"Find anything?" I asked, checking out the dresser and wondering if it was the one they'd bought from Cody.

"This rug. The placement is odd."

"You think it's covering something?" Bending down, I lifted one edge. "There's something under here."

"Well, it can't be dust bunnies. Claire keeps this place spotless." Doris was right. For all the heavy dust and grime in the barn, there wasn't a speck of either in the farmhouse.

Pulling the rug all the way back, we stood looking at what I'd exposed, both silent as we took it in. Burned into the wooden floorboards was a pentacle.

"What are we dealing with here?" It was rhetorical. Clearly, we were dealing with some sort of sorcery. "Are they witches?"

"They're something, that's for sure," Doris said, replacing the carpet and covering up the pentacle. "But so far, I'm not finding anything that could incriminate them for murder."

While Doris searched the closet, I opened the bathroom door. Not much to see—a pretty standard bathroom, but the mirrored cabinet above the sink caught my attention. One thing that struck me about the Whelans' home was that not only was it clean, it was tidy. Everything had a home. But the cabinet door sat ajar.

Curious, I approached, opening it farther to peek inside. Finding nothing out of the ordinary, I swung it shut, and that's when I noticed it. Or rather, lack of it. I was looking directly into a mirror, only I had no reflection. Now either I'd died and didn't know about it and was now a ghost—or a vampire—or there was something funky going on with the mirror.

"Doris?" I called.

"What's up?" She appeared in the bathroom doorway, and I pointed to the mirror. "There's no reflection."

"A trick mirror?"

"How would that work? Look, you can see the room but not me or you. Enchanted?"

We were standing in front of it, twisting this way and that, when Claire Whelan suddenly appeared in the mirror. A thick mist began to fill the room, and the scent of sulfur burned my nostrils.

"Demon," I hissed, swinging the mirrored door to angle it away from us. "We need to get out of here, now!"

Doris didn't need telling twice. She plunged an elbow into my ribs as she shoved me out of the way and hightailed it out the door. Regaining my balance, I hurried as fast as I could after her, taking care to close the back door after us and remove any trace that we'd been here at all. I didn't know if Claire had seen us or not, or if the mirror was some sort of portal or scrying tool, but I wasn't keen to hang around and find out.

Doris had the motor running by the time I reached the car. No sooner had I climbed in than she was tearing down the driveway, gravel spitting from beneath the tires. Of the Whelans, there was no sign.

"We need to ward our houses. You got salt?" I panted, breathless from my half sprint to the car.

"Pft, do I have salt!" Doris declared, then cleared her throat. "Actually, we might want to pass by the general store and stock up."

"You know, if it wasn't for the odor, I wouldn't have pegged them as demons. Well, Claire at least." I hadn't seen Beau in the mirror, but that's not to say he wasn't a demon.

"I've been in a demon's den before, and believe me, it didn't look anything like that farmhouse," Doris said.

"Same." There hadn't been a demonic statue or

velvet curtain in sight. "We're going to need holy water."

Doris patted her purse that sat wedged in the center console. "Taken care of."

My mouth dropped open. "Don't tell me you go to church every Sunday to replenish your supply of holy water?" I gasped. "That's genius, actually."

She shrugged one shoulder. "Don't tell Father O'Mally."

"I guess, given the ley line situation in Gravestone, warding your home makes sense." After all, if I was hiding out here, there was a fair chance that members of the SIA's most wanted list had hidden out here a time or two as well. Demons included.

"Oh, no, I don't use it for warding. I use it for my mint plant. It grows exceptionally well with a regular dose of holy water," Doris explained, reaching the end of the driveway, slowing just enough to check for oncoming traffic before flooring it onto the highway and heading back to Gravestone like a bat out of hell. She didn't slow down until we reached the town's city limits, and for once, I was grateful for Doris's need for speed. The sooner I got home and warded the house, the better. It hadn't escaped me that I'd left Flynn there, alone and unprotected, and if Claire Whelan had seen me through the mirror, she could be at my house already.

Doris slowed to a sedate pace as we made our way down the high street. I was watching out the side window when I saw Keelan. "Slow down," I hissed to Doris.

She immediately took her foot off the gas. "What's up?" Then she saw what I'd seen. Keelan Moore arguing with another man. An older, bald man. "Who's that?" I asked, although I was pretty sure I already knew the answer.

"That's Dino Cittadino arguing with Keelan Moore," Doris said, smoothly pulling off the road and gliding to a halt. Apparently, she could drive sedately when it suited her. We watched from the car as the two men continued their heated discussion. There was finger pointing, snarling, then Keelan shoved Dino in the chest and Dino punched Keelan in the jaw. Both men went down in a tangle of limbs before none other than Kerris Jones, mayor of Gravestone, broke it up.

She stood over them, gesturing angrily. Both men sheepishly climbed to their feet while the mayor continued to lambast them. Keelan spun on his heel and stalked off while Dino remained talking with the mayor. Color me surprised when, finished ranting, Kerris smiled and placed her hand on Dino's back in an almost comforting gesture before they walked away. *Together*.

"What on earth did we just witness?" It was a rhetorical question, but Doris answered anyway.

"It wouldn't surprise me in the least if Kerris is in business with Dino. He's a thug. He's just her speed."

And that's when Kerris's head snapped around, and her eyes landed on us, sitting in the Impala, watching her.

"Drive! Drive!"

Doris didn't need telling twice. She peeled away with a squeal of tires, leaving a trail of smoke and rubber. I clutched the door handle in terror. "Doris," I wheezed, trying to catch my breath. "Take it easy. We're trying *not* to draw attention, remember?"

"Right, right. Man, but that was fun though, huh?" Doris had a grin from ear to ear, but her foot barely budged from the accelerator. I couldn't relax. Nor could I unfurl my fingers from their death grip on the door handle. We flew along Porter Road and onto the Esplanade, where Doris yanked on the handbrake and drifted the car sideways into a parking space in front of the general store.

Fumbling, I released the seat belt and toppled out of the car.

"What's wrong with you?" Doris asked, trotting

around the hood to stand looking at me as I heaved and panted on the sidewalk.

"Your driving is what's wrong with me." Straightening, I placed a hand over my beating heart, trying to settle it into a more comfortable rhythm. "I think I'd prefer to come face-to-face with the Whelans in demon form than ride with you."

"That's not very polite," Doris said. "But also, you're not the first person who's said that. Not about the Whelans being demons but about not wanting to drive with me. Never mind. You survived, you're all in one piece, no harm, no foul." She slapped me on the back with the strength of a linebacker, and I almost face planted into the sidewalk.

"Come on, stop dilly dallying." She headed into the store, seemingly oblivious to her own strength. Slowly, I followed, cautiously rotating my shoulders, checking for injury.

Grabbing a cart, Doris headed straight for the spice section and cleared out the shelves. Twenty-four boxes of Morton table salt.

"You need anything?" she asked.

"Milk."

With our cart loaded with twenty-four packets of salt and one gallon of milk, we headed to check out.

"Afternoon, Doris." The man behind the counter straightened from where he'd been reading a Wired magazine with a picture of Elon Musk on the cover, casually tossing it beneath the counter. "Whatcha got there? That's an awful lot of salt."

"Hi, Howie. Holly here has a broken foot, and we heard that salt has healing powers, so we figured we'd soak her foot in it." She lied so smoothly, I almost believed her myself.

"Right-e-oh." Howie didn't bat an eye, just began scanning the boxes of salt. "Holly, eh? So, you're John Smith's niece?"

"He's my great uncle, yes."

Doris frowned, looking from me to Howie and back again. "You two haven't met?"

"I've been into the general store a couple of times now," I explained, "but didn't see Howie until today."

"You must've been served by Esther, my wife." Howie grinned. "Allow me to introduce myself. Howie Vasive, at your service."

I had to suck my lips in to keep from laughing. *How evasive?* Releasing my lips with a pop, I said with a straight face, "Pleasure to meet you, Howie."

"So, how did you bust your foot?"

"Fell out of bed."

He paused in scanning the salt to shoot me an incredulous look. I shrugged. "I know, I know, it sounds ridiculous." Because it was. "The navicular is a tiny bone in the middle of your foot, and all you need to do is put weight on it at just the wrong angle and snap." I clicked my fingers to demonstrate.

"You don't say?" Howie resumed ringing us up. He was a short man, balding, with a round belly and watery eyes behind his black frame glasses. I pegged him to be late fifties. The last time I'd been in the store, a woman who looked remarkably similar to Howie had served me. If he hadn't told me they were married, I would have taken them as siblings.

"That'll be a hundred and fifty dollars." He smiled, waiting for Doris to pay. When she made no move to do so, he shifted his gaze to me.

"Fine. I'll get it." Nudging Doris out of the way, I dutifully paid, trying not to wince. Harding was going to have a fit when he saw my expense report.

"You're the one with the inheritance. Plus, it's your busted foot," Doris pointed out, grabbing one of the bags Howie had packed from the counter, clutching it to her chest as she grappled with the weight.

"Let me help you out to the car with these," Howie offered, grabbing another bag, leaving me with the last one. Out at the car, Doris shoved her bag into my arms while she popped the trunk.

"Is that… scuba gear?" In the trunk, there appeared to be an oxygen tank, fins, a mask, and what could only be a wetsuit screwed up into a ball.

"Yeah." Doris shrugged in a so-what manner. "Just dump 'em in."

We placed the bags in the trunk, and Doris slammed it shut. "So I like to do a little diving in my spare time. So what?"

"Nothing. It just hadn't occurred to me that a woman of your…" I bit my lip, casting around for the right word. Doris crossed her arms and glared, daring me to continue.

"Caliber?" Howie offered.

"Yes, exactly." I smiled at Howie. "That a woman of your *caliber* partakes in scuba diving."

"I'm a woman of many talents," Doris declared. "Thanks, Howie. Say hi to Esther for me." She patted him on the shoulder with bone crushing enthusiasm, then slid behind the wheel. "Come on, Holly, we have salting to do."

"Right." I hobbled to the passenger side and opened the door. "Thanks, Howie. Sorry we cleaned out your salt supply."

Howie waved. "No problem. We always seem to go through a lot of salt. Dunno why that is." He mumbled the latter to himself as he headed back inside.

"Are they always open?" I asked Doris, pulling on my seatbelt.

"Oh, yeah. Seven days."

"So, no church then?"

"Not for Howie. Esther goes. She has Sundays off from the store, Howie has Mondays off. The rest of the week, they're on together, so you're likely to run into one or the other."

"Howie mentioned they sell a lot of salt. Do you think that's because people know about the Whelans? That Beau and Claire are demons, and they're warding their houses? Are Howie and Esther witches too?"

"What is this, twenty questions?"

"Curious minds want to know," I protested. It was a short drive to my house on Berryman Street, and we were already pulling up out front.

"I didn't know Beau and Claire were demons,"

Doris said, shutting off the engine and pulling the keys from the ignition. Before getting out, she turned to me. "You can't tell anyone. They've lived here a couple of years, recently got married. I suspect they're hiding out, just like you."

"Yeah, but if she saw us through the mirror, she knows we were at their place. They're bound to come looking for us."

"Which is why we have the salt."

"And after all that, we didn't find anything they could have used as a weapon to kill Cody." It had been a long shot, though.

"Could be in their car." Doris popped the trunk, then opened the door and climbed out. I followed suit.

"Or thrown out the window halfway between Gravestone and their farm." Searching the farm had been a fruitless exercise. And we hadn't really searched it, not properly. And honestly, I didn't know what I'd been thinking. Searching a farm was a huge undertaking, and considering we didn't even know what, exactly, we were searching for? "We need to plan better," I mumbled under my breath, reaching into the trunk for one of the paper bags.

"We need to find out what they told Calder," Doris said, heaving a bag onto her hip and following me to the front door. "Find out what their alibi is."

"You think he's going to tell us?"

"He might tell you. He's taken a bit of a liking to you."

I could feel the blood rush up my neck and into my cheeks. Keeping my back to Doris so she couldn't see, I shouldered open the front door and headed through the house to the kitchen at the back.

"Flynn?" A quick search proved he wasn't in the house, which had my heart skipping a beat in panic until I realized how stiflingly hot it was inside. Flinging open the back door to allow some cross breeze, I fired up the pedestal fan in a fruitless attempt to cool the house.

"When are you going to get Casey to install AC?" Doris fanned her face, sweat beading on her weathered skin. It had to be hot for Doris to be complaining.

"Sooner rather than later." I'd been thinking I'd get it installed when I formalized the renovations I had planned, but with the oppressive heat unrelenting, I was rapidly changing my mind. Especially with the amount of baking I did. I'd sacrificed comfort for baked goods, but if I wanted to keep us safe and out of the clutches of any demons, we'd need to install a cooling system to make staying in the house bearable. A single unit in the living room would be better than the whole lot of nothing I had going on right now. Pulling out my phone, I shot Casey a message to have him call me when he was free.

Doris began unpacking the salt while I stepped out onto the back porch. Cupping my hands around my mouth, I yelled, "Flynn!" There was rustling in the leaves of the cedar elm tree, and seconds later, a streak of purple came hurtling down the tree, across the yard, and up my leg.

"Cooler up there, huh?" I asked as he settled into his favorite spot on my shoulder. "So, we went out to the Whelans' farm, and I'm pretty sure they're demons," I told him. His grip on my hair tightened, and I reached up to pat him. "It's okay. They weren't home. But Doris says they're probably hiding out like us. There haven't been any demon attacks in Gravestone, so they're definitely flying under the radar, but just to be safe, we've got a truckload of salt and are laying down wards."

Flynn squeaked in response.

"Also, I'm going to talk to Casey about getting AC installed in the house. Until the Whelan situation is resolved, I don't want you hanging around outside on your own. Stay inside where I know you'll be safe." If I was hot, I could only imagine how hot Flynn was with a fur coat.

Stepping back into the house, I grabbed the milk off the counter and put it away in the fridge. "How much salt do you need?" I asked Doris. "Do you have any at home?"

"I think I've got one packet," she said. "Let's go halfsies. If either of us needs more…"

"One packet should do this entire house," I pointed out. We had twenty-four packets. Even if Doris took twelve of them, I still had more than enough.

"Yeah, but you gotta keep it topped up. Break the

seal and you've got to put more down. Every door and window."

"I know."

Delving into her purse, she pulled out a water bottle. Unscrewing the lid, she inserted her finger in the top, then drew a symbol on the back door. It dried within seconds. She repeated the process with the front door. "There," she declared, putting the lid back on the water and dropping it in her purse. "That should hold you. Remember, if the door gets wet, or you decide to do something crazy like paint it, we need to ward it again."

"Thankfully, both doors are sheltered from the rain, but I'll bear it in mind."

Dusting off her hands, she picked up the paper bag containing her share of the salt. "I'm heading home to ward my house again. Can't be too careful."

"Okay. Call me later?"

"Sure."

As soon as Doris left, I grabbed a packet of salt, tore it open, and laid a trail across the front and back doorsteps, then every window-sill in the house. And I was right. I'd used precisely one packet of salt. Shoving the remaining packets in the cupboard with my jars of flour, I was contemplating having another go at the puzzle box when a knock sounded at the front door. For a second, my heart leaped into my throat thinking the Whelans had arrived to demand to know what I'd been doing trespassing at their farm today.

Walking through the living room, I breathed a sigh of relief when I spotted Casey's silhouette through the screen door.

"Oh, hey." I smiled, pushing the door open and inviting him inside. He stepped over the line of salt, one brow raised. "Ants." I lied.

"Phew." He wiped his brow with his forearm. "Sure is a hot one."

"Which is why I messaged you." I led the way back to the kitchen, opening the fridge and grabbing a soda. "You didn't need to drop by, though. A call would have been fine. Soda?"

"Sure." He nodded, and I tossed him one. "I was in the neighborhood. Figured I'd drop in, see how you're doing. You want to talk about the renovations?"

"That and I really need an AC installed, Casey."

"Agreed. I'm surprised old John didn't have one put in already."

"Me too." It was crazy, given that Gravestone was hot three-hundred-and-sixty-five days a year. But today was exceptional. Today felt like we were living on the sun.

"I've got an old one I can temporarily rig up in the window of your living room," Casey offered. "It'll get you by until we get the renovations done. Speaking of, you wanna see what I've come up with so far?"

"That temporary AC sounds perfect, and yes, please show me what you've got." The sooner I signed off on the plans, the sooner we could begin work and make the house more habitable. Murphy's Law dictated that as soon as that was done, I'd be out of here, and that day couldn't come fast enough. I was chomping at the bit to return to work.

We sat together at the kitchen table, and Casey flicked through the sketches he'd drawn on his phone. "I think if we knock out this wall between the kitchen and living room but keep the mud room, cos we need that wall for structural integrity, we can open this right up. Reconfigure the kitchen layout so you won't end up with a refrigerator in the living room space. Put in a split system air conditioning system that can service the open area downstairs and the master bedroom upstairs. Upstairs, structurally, we'll keep the same layout, modernize the bathroom, lick of paint in the bedrooms, possibly new flooring depending on what I find when I rip up the carpet. What do you think?"

"I think that sounds perfect." And I honestly didn't care about the cost because it would be going on the SIA's tab. Call it payback for sequestering me here for goodness knows how long, unable to use my magic. And if my boss, Scott Harding, had a problem with it, he could bite me. I'd had zero contact with the agency since arriving here days ago. I'd never been forced into hiding before and so far, wasn't a fan. But my cover story was sound, and I could pass off the expense of the renovations as using my fictional inheritance from my fake great uncle, John Smith.

It was kinda exciting going through the plans with Casey. We were talking paint colors and tile selections when a knock sounded at the front door. Considering I was new in town and barely knew anyone, I wasn't expecting visitors. Although the possibility that the Whelans would show up on my doorstep immediately pushed its way to the forefront of my mind yet again. Would they knock, though? Can you imagine two angry demons turning up on your doorstep to demand to know why you were trespassing on their property, only they're polite enough to knock before tearing you apart?

Turns out it wasn't the Whelans. Sheriff Joshua Calder stood on my stoop, hat in hand.

"Calder," I greeted, opening the screen door and waving him inside. He eyed the line of salt. "Ants." He nodded, totally buying the lie, just like Casey had.

"Come on through," I invited. "I'm just going over some renovation plans with Casey. Soda?"

"Please." Calder followed me into the kitchen, saw Casey sitting at my kitchen table, and gave him a look I couldn't read. Both men greeted each other with a nod of the head, and the testosterone level in the room skyrocketed.

"Um." Casey looked from me to Calder and back again. "Why don't I head out and grab that old AC for you, Holly? It won't take me long to wedge it in the window."

"That'd be great. Thanks, Casey. Flynn will be most grateful to get a decent night's sleep too."

"Yeah, it must be super hot for the poor little fella." Casey stood, the kitchen feeling impossibly small with the two men in it. "I'll be back soon. The air-con is back at my workshop."

"Sure, thanks, Casey." I smiled, grateful for his help.

After Casey had left, one thing was apparent. The heat in the kitchen had just intensified, and it had nothing to do with the temperature.

CHAPTER
Eight

"How about that soda?" Calder drawled, tossing his hat onto the counter, his hazel eyes looking impossibly green this afternoon.

"Sure." Opening the fridge, I grabbed a soda and handed it to him, our fingers brushing. Electricity shot up my arm, and I snatched my hand away.

"What brings you by?" I asked, only my voice came out an octave higher than usual. Clearing my throat, I reclaimed my seat at the table. I waved at the empty chair opposite, and Calder eased himself down, not taking his eyes off me.

"I need to ask you about what you witnessed at the market yesterday," he said. "Between Beau and Claire Whelan and Cody Pendant. Given what happened at the crime scene this morning, I figured you wouldn't be particularly keen on coming down to the station to answer questions, so I came to you."

I actually appreciated the gesture. It was thoughtful.

Or maybe it was a ploy to lull me into a false sense of security. I couldn't be sure. Leaning back in my chair, I studied him. While Casey was cover model gorgeous and a good ten years younger than Calder, if not more, Calder definitely wasn't lacking in terms of attractiveness. Calder was what I'd call ruggedly handsome, from his chiseled jaw to the five o'clock shadow to the laugh lines. He had hard edges and exuded an air of authority that was impossible to deny. While Casey was certainly manly, Calder practically screamed alpha.

"Right," I finally acknowledged what he'd said. But rather than answer his question, I asked one of my own. "What did the Whelans tell you?"

"What do you think they told me?"

"Are we just going to play twenty questions and not actually answer anything?" I shot back. The problem was, I wasn't sure who I could trust. And I badly wanted to trust Calder. Yet… it was murky. I'd been given strict instructions to avoid local law enforcement. Considering I'd been thrown in jail twice, we could safely say I'd failed at that particular assignment.

"What's going on in that head of yours?" Calder drawled, the gravelly tone of his voice oddly soothing. If I didn't know better, I could have sworn he was using some sort of enchantment over me. But that was impossible because Sheriff Joshua Calder was human. And I was not.

"What do you mean?" I hedged, shifting uncomfortably in my seat.

"Why don't you just tell me whatever it is that's on your mind and we'll take it from there, hmm?"

If only it were that easy. How much did Calder know about the SIA and the paranormals currently residing in Gravestone? He knew something, Doris had indicated as much, and when he'd arrested the crazy witch who'd hexed Seth Saltzman to death, he hadn't batted an eye. I knew local law enforcement often worked with the SIA, but until I could confirm Calder's status with Harding, I couldn't risk saying anything. But maybe I could pass on information that wasn't supernatural in nature?

"Sorry. My thought process is somewhat fried today. It's the heat."

"But Casey is taking care of that for you, correct? He's gone to get an AC right now."

I nodded. "Yes. He has."

Calder glanced around the room, taking in the peeling paint, the torn linoleum, one of the cupboard doors barely hanging on. "I'm surprised John didn't keep this place in better repair."

"Aren't we all?" I'd heard over and over that John Smith was a brilliant carpenter, but you wouldn't know it judging by his house. It was a strong wind away from being derelict. But despite the home's appearances, Casey had inspected the foundation and declared the house to be structurally sound.

"Did you enjoy the market?" Calder changed tacks. I knew it. He knew it. Yet I didn't call him on it.

"I did. Although I didn't stay long. With the storm

approaching, I bought some flour and came home to do some baking."

"What did you bake?"

"Bread."

"Bread?" He sounded surprised.

I nodded. "Yes. Bread. The stuff you make sandwiches with."

"Or toast."

I smiled a little. "Or toast. Look, I didn't see much at the market—between the Whelans and Cody. I was grabbing a funnel cake with Doris at River's stall. We heard an altercation and saw the Whelans arguing with Cody. Then the Whelans left."

I wondered if Cody had known the young couple he'd ripped off were demons? Surely not. He wouldn't be so brazen as to rip off a demon, would he? The thing was, I didn't think they'd killed him. Why would a demon knock you over the head? They had much more efficient ways of killing you. That's if they wanted you dead. If I'd been in their position, I would have exacted a very different revenge. One that included itching powder in underwear. Night terrors. A long and protracted torment.

"Then you went to Cody's stall and bought the puzzle box." Calder dragged me out of my murderous fantasy.

"Yep. I did. Macey sold it to me." But Calder already knew this.

"But apparently it wasn't for sale."

I shrugged. "It was on the table with the other items.

I didn't steal it." This was starting to feel like an inquisition, and I didn't like it. Not one bit. Seemed like Calder realized he'd taken a wrong turn, too.

"I wasn't suggesting that you did." His voice was soothing, and I narrowed my eyes. Was he trying to play me? Emphasis on the trying. We'd already established I didn't steal the puzzle box, so I wasn't sure why it kept coming up.

"What is it you're getting at? Stop dancing around the question and just ask," I snapped, annoyance level rising sharply.

"Did you kill Cody Pendant?" he asked bluntly.

"No, I did not," I shot back.

He smiled. "That's what I thought."

"But you had to ask."

"I had to ask," he agreed. "There were witnesses to your altercation with Cody over the puzzle box."

"Of course there was. I've got nothing to hide. I bought it fair and square. He claimed it wasn't for sale, and look, if he hadn't been such an aggressive douche about it, I'd have probably given it back. But he was, so I didn't. Anyway, someone broke in here last night, and I suspect they were after the box."

He froze for a split second before placing his elbows on the table and leaning toward me. "Say what now?"

I rolled my eyes. "It's fine. I'm fine. Someone jimmied my back door in the middle of the night."

He shot up and strode to the back door, examining the deep scratches etched into the frame. "And you think they were after the puzzle box?"

I shrugged. "I don't know. They were upstairs in the front bedroom, which is empty except for the bookcase, so maybe they were after something else entirely. Which reminds me, I was supposed to get a bolt for the door today, and I forgot."

"Casey probably has something in his truck that'll do the job," he pointed out, then, before I could stop him, Calder headed upstairs, I assumed to check on the front bedroom. Seconds later, he was back.

"They tossed the room." He resumed his seat across from me.

"Actually, I think that was Flynn. I'm pretty sure he went up to investigate the noises and probably startled the intruder. I assume they bumped into the bookcase and the whole thing toppled."

"Where were you when all this happened?"

"I was asleep." I jerked my thumb toward the living room, my temporary bedroom. "Creaking floorboards woke me. I was at the foot of the stairs when the bookcase went over. That's when the intruder fled. Obviously, if I hadn't already heard them, the crashing of the bookcase would have alerted me, so they bolted."

"Did you see them?"

"Not clearly. They pushed me into the wall as they ran past. Dressed all in black from head to toe, baggy, loose clothing with a hoodie covering their head. I didn't see their face at all."

"Male? Female?"

"Honestly couldn't say. Average. Everything about them was average. Average build, average height. I know, you don't need to tell me that isn't much to go on. Which is why I didn't bother reporting it. I can't give you a decent description of the intruder, therefore, you've got nothing to go on. All you could do is fill out a report, and paperwork isn't going to help anybody." And the last thing I needed was more paperwork with my name on it.

He sat back, arms crossed over his chest, a deep frown pulling his brows down low. I could feel a lecture coming on.

"Do you think the Whelans killed Cody?" I asked, in an attempt to head him off.

"Why? Do you?"

Irritation pricked my skin, making me itch. "Honestly? No, I don't. But I'm about done having a conversation with you if you answer every one of my questions with one of your own. This isn't a formal interview. According to you, I'm not a suspect. So, this —" I pointed from myself to him "—is a two-way street. If you want to talk with me, then talk. If not, it's time for you to go." I was amazed at my own audacity. Kicking the sheriff out for asking questions. I thought I heard Flynn squeak from the other room but couldn't be sure. Probably laughing his ass off.

Calder studied me in silence for a long, hot minute. I held his gaze, losing myself in the depths of his eyes. He had really lovely eyes, the hazel green color accentuated with flecks of gold, the lashes dark and thick. We stared at each other, the silence broken only by the creaks emitted by the old house. I was used to them now. Kind of. It was quiet living out here, no neighbors, no traffic. The first couple of nights in this house, I'd barely slept, not used to the quiet, nor the sounds coming from the mangroves bordering my back yard. Funny how quickly you get used to it.

Calder startled me by pulling out his phone, scrolling through the screen before holding it out toward me. "Do you recognize this?"

I dragged my gaze from his to the phone, then realized what I was looking at. Taking the phone from him, I peered at the image on the screen. It was my name and address, written on a scrap of paper. There was a brown smudge in one corner.

"Is this the note that was in Cody's hand?"

"Yes."

The smudge was his blood. "It's not my handwriting. I didn't write it." I passed the phone back.

"It's not Cody's handwriting either." Calder placed the phone on the table, resting his fingers on top of it. "So the question is, who wrote it and why did they give it to Cody?"

"You think maybe it's to do with my break-in? But I have to be honest, I don't think it was Cody. The build was all wrong."

"How about Macey? He could have sent her to do his bidding."

"Possibly. I couldn't say definitively. The clothing they were wearing was loose. Like sweatpants. So, it could have been a woman." It irked me to no end, not being able to identify if my intruder had even been male or female.

"What can you tell me about the puzzle box?"

I shook my head, huffing out a sigh. "Nothing much, other than it's a puzzle box. I haven't been able to get it open."

Calder appeared to be deep in thought, drumming his fingers on the phone. "We need to get the box authenticated, see if it is an antique and therefore valuable."

"And who do you suggest does that?"

"Honestly? I don't know. Let me do some research and get back to you. Perhaps I should take the box with me? Lock it up at the station for safe keeping?"

The icy chill that slithered up my spine and wrapped itself around my heart was not pleasant. I knew my mouth was opening and closing like a fish flopping on the shore, but words failed me. I had not been expecting Calder to want the box. To say I was highly suspicious of his motives was an understatement. Not to mention the last time Calder had taken evidence from my house, it had been stolen from under his nose.

"No need. It's in a safe place."

"Oh? Where?"

I snorted. "We've established that I didn't steal it, and therefore, legally, it's mine. Is it really any concern of law enforcement where it is?"

"It's at the center of a murder investigation," he pointed out. "I think so."

"You don't know that. You're going to have to trust me on this. It's safe. And unless you can get a warrant forcing me to hand it over, it stays with me."

Moments passed before he inclined his head and gave me one of those slow, sexy smiles that threatened to buckle my knees. If only I could trust him.

"Fair enough." He stood, and I automatically followed suit, trailing him to the front door. Stepping over the line of salt without disturbing it, he stood on the stoop, one hand holding the screen door open while he turned back to me. "You can trust me," he said, voice low, like he'd been chewing nails.

"Can I?" I wished with all my heart that I could, but the truth was, I wasn't sure. And that, apparently, rankled both of us.

CHAPTER
Nine

"This is much better, right, Flynn?" I was sitting in the camp chair in the living room, the AC Casey had jammed in the window rattling and rumbling louder than a truck engine but never-the-less churning out blessedly cool air. Flynn was stretched out on my camp bed directly in front of the vents. I figured he'd earned a little cool air pampering and let him take prime position.

Opening my laptop, I checked my emails. Harding had said he'd contact me at the dummy address we'd setup if he had any news. So far, my inbox remained empty.

"You know, maybe I should have told Calder about Keelan Moore," I said to Flynn, who lay watching me. "And what River had told us about Dino Cittadino threatening Cody?" But that would have dropped River in it, and she was already mad at me. But then again, if Calder was working with the SIA, then he probably already knew about the Tarkath Syndicate, and if he was any sort of lawman, he'd know Dino worked for them.

"I wonder if Keelan is with the Tarkaths too?" I typed Keelan's name in a search engine, but nothing came up. Not for the Keelan Moore I was searching for, anyway. "I wish I could log in to my SIA account," I grumbled. But Harding had locked me out. It was for my own safety, he'd said. If there was a mole in the SIA, then they'd be able to track me as soon as I logged in. Hence being locked out. That's when Flynn's head popped up and his ears wriggled. "What?"

Standing up, he scampered to the end of the cot, jumped across to the chair where I was sitting, and wriggled himself onto my lap. I watched as he ran back and forth across the keyboard, then gasped when the login for the SIA server appeared on the screen.

"Oh my God!" I breathed. "You have access? Why didn't they revoke it?" Probably because he was a rat, and they didn't factor in he'd have the skill set required to login. Plus, no one knew he was with me. Revoking Flynn's access hadn't been on their radar.

Flynn ignored me as he typed in his credentials, and a second later, the SIA logo appeared on the screen. We were in. Flynn scrambled up to my shoulder, watching as I typed in Keelan Moore's name. Sure enough, his profile appeared, confirming Keelan was of interest to the SIA. And no wonder. Keelan Moore was a member of the Arzan Brotherhood, not the Tarkath Syndicate like I'd suspected.

"Keelan is with the Arzans," I said to Flynn. "Who are in direct competition with the Tarkaths. Only the Arzans' magic comes from artifacts, whereas the Tarkaths' comes from the powers of their ancestors. Members of the Arzan Brotherhood are sent far and wide to source relics that will benefit their cause." My thoughts immediately went to the puzzle box. "Do you think the puzzle box is actually an artifact, and I got it wrong?"

But Flynn squeaked and shook his head.

"No? So, maybe an artifact is inside? We really need to get that box open." I finished skimming Keelan's record. "We can confirm Keelan Moore is a member of the Arzan Brotherhood. Equally as dangerous as the Tarkaths. Equally bad news. Two rival gangs. Is this a turf war? But given Gravestone's unique ability to hide magic, surely it's considered Switzerland. Is Gravestone a neutral meeting place between two warring factions? Neither could dominate here. And yet two members of opposing gangs happened to be in Gravestone at the same time, and an antique dealer who deals in black market occult items happens to turn up dead? Definitely not a coincidence." Closing the laptop, I laid it on the floor and stood.

"Come on, it's time to get this puzzle box open once and for all." Limping into the kitchen, I retrieved the box, tucking it under my arm. Sliding open the bolt Casey had installed on the back door, I thumped my way down the steps and headed toward John Smith's garage. The sun was setting, the temperature outside somewhat bearable, but gray clouds gathered overhead, and in the distance, thunder rumbled.

Flynn darted ahead of me, and by the time I reached the garage, he was already sitting on the dust-covered workbench at the rear. Placing the puzzle box on the workbench, I stood back to examine the tools hanging on the pegboard above it. I needed something I could use to wedge into one of the movable pieces of the box and pry it open. Or maybe the handsaw? Just cut the whole thing in half? While I was pondering my choices, Flynn was messing around with the box, sniffing it and running his little paws all over it. I didn't pay him much attention. If I couldn't crack the code, he couldn't. Only, of course, he did. There was a click and a sliding noise and Flynn's triumphant squeak.

"Oh my God, you did it!"

A loud crack of thunder sounded directly overhead a split second before rain hit the ground in a torrential downpour. "This has to be the hottest, wettest place on Earth," I said, watching as the deluge hammered down, the sound of it on the tin roof deafening. Then I turned my attention back to the puzzle box. Flynn had found the trigger, and all it took was me sliding the top back to reveal what was inside. Heads together, we peered into the box.

"Wow."

Squeak.

Reaching in, I pulled out a diamond shaped, blue crystal. Holding it up, we examined it. "This is definitely what Keelan is after," I said. Flynn nodded in agreement, then began squeaking and waving his paws around.

"I assume you're saying we should take this inside and do some research, find out exactly what we're dealing with?"

He nodded, then began pushing the puzzle box closed. Before he closed it completely, I picked up a rock and placed it inside.

"The rock should weigh about the same as the crystal. We don't want anyone to know we got it open." Sliding the crystal into my pocket, I picked up the puzzle box and closed it, sealing the rock inside. Ducking my head, I stepped out into the downpour. "Meet you inside," I yelled over the roar of the rain. Flynn bolted ahead of me, and by the time I reached the back door, I was soaked to the skin.

"Should've thought to bring a towel down from the bathroom," I said to Flynn, who sat in a puddle, a bedraggled mess. "But then, I wasn't expecting it to rain yet." Despite the dark clouds, I'd thought we'd had a bit of time before the heavens opened. Wringing as much water out of my hair as I could, I opened the back door and stepped inside, my walking boot squelching. Placing the puzzle box on the counter, I locked the back door and slid the newly installed bolt into place. Flynn darted up the stairs ahead of me, already sitting in the bathroom sink when I arrived.

Grabbing the spare towel, I rubbed him down, leaving his fur standing on end in sharp spikes. I couldn't help but giggle. "Looking good," I assured him, giving him the thumbs up. He shot me a look of disdain and jumped down from the sink. I waited until he'd left the bathroom before I peeled my wet clothes off, leaving them in a sodden heap on the floor.

After a quick shower, I wrapped myself in a towel and wrestled with the pocket of the soaked dress to retrieve the crystal. The light bounced off it, casting shards of ice blue around the bathroom. "You're very pretty," I said to it, "but what do you do? You must do something for a member of the Arzan to want you. Are you a relic?"

The crystal twinkled in the light and said absolutely nothing. Which was exactly what I expected from an inanimate object. Drying off my walking boot as best as I could, I left it in the hallway to finish drying while I got dressed in shorts and a tee in the back bedroom. Carrying the crystal downstairs, I was surprised to discover Flynn had gotten the laptop open and was furiously running across the keyboard, typing.

Taking a seat on the cot, I waited until he was done before picking the laptop up off the floor. "What's this?"

Flynn jumped up next to me, reading with me what was on the screen.

"It *is* an artifact. The soul stone. Odd that they'd call it a stone when it's technically a crystal," I said. Flynn shrugged in a *whatever* gesture. "So, what does it do, this soul stone? Resurrect the dead? Collect souls?"

Flynn pointed farther down the page, and I zeroed in on the words. "Oh, it's a conduit. It amplifies magic. No wonder the Arzan Brotherhood wants it."

According to the website, the soul stone had been missing for years, stolen from a shrine in Malaysia, never to be seen again. Its monetary value in human terms was nothing much, a few hundred dollars, but to the supernatural world, the soul stone was priceless. And in the wrong hands, it could blow the lid off Gravestone's little secret, and the ley line that hid magic could potentially be destroyed. I figured there would be a lot of people who wouldn't want that to happen. Enough to kill Cody to stop the soul stone from changing hands? It was a distinct possibility.

The following morning, I was checking that the salt around the doors and windows remained unbroken when I received a message from Casey that he'd submitted my renovation plans to the council for a permit and that, in the meantime, he'd order in supplies. I couldn't contain my eye roll. "What's the bet Kerris will try to block it?" I said to Flynn, who looked at me with a blank expression before scratching behind his ear. Kerris Jones had offered me an obscene amount of money to buy this house and had been furious when I'd declined. I figured it had something to do with the mangrove boardwalk she had planned, the boardwalk that John Smith had vehemently opposed when he'd been alive and one that I'd decided to look into with greater detail.

My phone dinged again, only this time the message was from Doris.

"How's the ward holding up?" she asked.

"All good here. You?" I replied.

"All good. Whatcha doing?"

"Sorting out books. Come over. Bring boxes." I'd been putting off sorting out John Smith's bookcases long enough. Now that Casey was moving forward with the renovation, I knew I'd have to sort out the mess the intruder had left behind sooner or later, and today seemed as good a day as any.

Most of John Smith's possessions had been dumped. Sadly, they were of little to no value, and I wondered at the life a man in his seventies had led to leave him with practically nothing at the end. There were only a handful of things left to sort out. The bookcase in the master bedroom, now strewn across the floor, and the bookcase in the living room. Then there was the shed out back. I figured I'd ask Casey if he wanted any of the tools, and as for the faded red and silver 1988 Chevrolet, I fully intended to make it roadworthy ASAP. Only problem, it was a stick shift, and I couldn't drive it with my broken foot. Hence the bicycle Doris had loaned me, which was awkward and cumbersome with the walking boot but came with a handy basket for Flynn to ride in.

I was in the kitchen, procrastinating over starting the clean-up job upstairs, when Doris's cheery, "Yoo-hoo!" reached my ears. Opening the front door, I was greeted with three cardboard boxes stacked on top of each other. I couldn't even see Doris behind them.

"Oh, good, you're home. Here. Take these. I've got more in the car."

Grabbing the boxes, I carried them inside, watching as Doris zipped back and forth between the Impala and the house. By the time she was done, I had a dozen boxes in my living room.

"AC is working great," Doris said, slamming the front door closed.

"Sure is. Wish I'd thought of it sooner." It would have been a godsend when I was baking, turning the hot house into an even hotter house, to have a little cool air circulating. "But be warned, it does not reach upstairs. The master bedroom is hot."

Hot was an understatement. It was hot *and* humid. Opening the windows in all the upstairs rooms to try and create a cross breeze had been wishful thinking. I was already sweating uncomfortably, and we hadn't even started sorting out the books yet.

"Maybe this is a job for an evening?" I sighed, wiping sweat out of my eyes. "When it's cooler."

"Nonsense. Between the two of us, we'll get this packed up in no time. They're only books, Holly, not the crown jewels."

What the crown jewels had to do with anything I didn't know, but I could hardly leave a little old lady to swelter alone, so I begrudgingly lowered myself to the floor, dragged a box close to my side, began picking up books, and, after a rudimentary glance, placing them in the box.

"I was thinking earlier that it's kinda sad John didn't really have much when he died. Like, mostly junk."

"You mean that he didn't leave behind some kind of legacy?" Doris didn't look up.

"Yeah, I guess." I hadn't really thought about what I'd leave behind when I died, but I was certainly hoping that wasn't anytime soon.

"You can take one man's trash to another man's treasure, but you can't make it drink," Doris said cryptically, and I snorted out a laugh at her mixed metaphor.

"He sure was an avid reader, though." I placed another book in the box.

"Eclectic tastes too. Looks like he's read every genre under the sun and then some. Not only fiction, but there are gardening books, books on astronomy, self-help books, health and fitness. He could start a small library."

"Speaking of, do you think the local library would want these?" The community library was a small affair, sharing space with the local school. I imagined they didn't have a big budget for books.

"Good idea." Doris was kneeling across from me, a book open on her knees.

"You know we're meant to be putting them in boxes, not reading them?" I teased. "What do you have there, anyway?"

She held up the book so I could read the title. "*The*

Beginner's Guide to Demonology," I read out loud. Then I connected the dots, gasping. "Holy heck. It can't be a coincidence, can it? We discover the Whelans are demons and now we find a book on demonology in John's collection." Had the old man known about the young couple's status?

Doris shrugged. "No idea. But let's keep this one." She put the book to one side.

"Agreed."

Within an hour, we had the books packed into five boxes that I'd dragged out onto the landing. "Do not even attempt to carry them down the stairs," I warned Doris when I caught her eyeing them. "I'll get Casey to do it. I'm sure he won't mind, and even if he does mind, I'll pay him extra to take care of it."

"Spoil sport," she huffed, but I could tell by the relieved droop of her shoulders that she hadn't been relishing carting the heavy boxes downstairs. "Is the coffee on?"

"The coffee is always on," I assured her, following her down the stairs. "Go wait in the living room where it's cool. I'll bring it through."

Pouring two cups of coffee, I carried them into the living room to find Doris sitting in the camp chair, the demonology book open in her lap. I handed her a cup before taking a seat on the camp bed.

"I take it it's an interesting read?" I asked, jerking my head toward the book.

"Fascinating. It's old. I came across a few demons

during my time with the SIA, but I had no idea there were so many species."

I shrugged. "What does it say about warding against them? Is the salt and holy water enough?" My SIA-issued pyre gun would have been ample protection, but since I was without it, I felt distinctly vulnerable.

"Haven't read anything that says different." She closed the book and tossed it onto the end of the camp bed. "We should do this bookcase, too. He may have some other gems hidden among the shelves."

"Are you sure? I don't want to impose. I'm sure there are other things you could be doing other than helping me pack up bookshelves."

"Not really. Calder said if I want to walk around naked, I have to do it inside."

I almost choked on my coffee. "What?"

"I know, right? You think I'd be able to water my garden in the nude if I wanted to, but noooo, Calder said there had been complaints and something about public indecency."

Biting my lip to keep from laughing, I nodded. "You also have to consider not getting sunburned on your… bits." I guess I should be grateful she'd turned up fully clothed.

"Always something to take into consideration."

CHAPTER

Ten

"I've been summoned." Straightening from where I'd been crouched in front of the big old bookcase in John Smith's living room, I placed a hand against my aching lower back and massaged the protesting muscles.

"Oh? Who by?" Doris, who sat crossed-legged on the floor next to me, eagerly perusing the leather-bound books she was pulling from the shelves, didn't bother looking up.

"None other than the mayor herself, Kerris Jones." I waggled my phone. The text message had arrived a few seconds ago.

"Kerris messaged you?" Doris sounded surprised. "I didn't know she'd know how."

I ignored her dig at Kerris's technical skills, or lack thereof. "Actually, it's from Casey. He submitted the plans to the council to get a permit for the renovations for this place. Apparently, Kerris told him that she *might* be able to fast track the process if I were to come down and meet with her personally."

"Ha!" Doris snorted. "By fast track, she means whack a rejected stamp on it and send you on your way. All that woman is interested in is everyone else's business and getting her own way."

"What's the bet she's going to offer to buy the house again?" I'd already rejected her offer once. Was she going to up the price? If the house were really mine, I'd be foolish to turn her down, but it wasn't, so I couldn't —but Kerris didn't know that. As it was, Harding was probably going to have a fit when he got the bill for the unauthorized renovations. Maybe that'd teach him a lesson for sending me here, forcing me into hiding rather than doing what I do best, hunting rogue paranormals.

"And since when is she personally involved in approving building permits?" Doris asked.

"Since my name is on it. I'm guessing it was flagged as soon as Casey submitted it." Holding out a hand, I hauled Doris to her feet. "Might as well get this over with. Can you drop me off?"

"Sure, it's almost time for the Keen Agers meeting, anyway. I'll drop you on my way."

The Keen Agers was the new community social group Doris had created. Initially, they'd been called the Women of Gravestone Committee. Only Kerris had muscled her way in and basically taken over the group, changing the rules and making everyone do her mayoral bidding. At my suggestion, Doris had broken rank, and Keen Agers was born. Rule number one, no one who worked for the council was allowed. So far, Kerris had not caught wind of the new group. We figured when she did, she wouldn't be pleased, especially when she learned that she didn't qualify for membership.

"Where are y'all meeting?"

"My house." She flung open the front door so hard it hit the wall and bounced back. "Get a wriggle on."

The council chambers were on Spencer Street and, like most businesses in Gravestone, had originally started out as an old house that had been refurbished into commercial space. With its sandstone exterior, complete with turrets and flagpole, the building was gorgeous, and stepping inside was like stepping back in time. Glistening wood, huge arched windows, plush carpet in a subtle royal blue, antique furniture from wall to wall —it screamed luxury mansion, not modern offices.

"Yes?" The receptionist behind the highly polished teak counter beckoned me forward. "How can I help you today?"

"My name is Holly Day," I managed to say without cringing. I hated my fictitious name with a passion. My real name was Tess Hunter, otherwise known as Twitch the Witch. "I believe Kerris wanted to see me."

"Kerris? You mean the mayor?" I didn't miss the censure in her tone but chose to ignore it. I knew all about the likes of Kerris Jones and their over-inflated egos, expecting all and sundry to bow down and worship the very ground they walked on.

"Yes. The mayor. Kerris Jones." I plastered on a fake smile and committed the cardinal sin of leaning my forearm along the countertop, marring the polish with my sweaty skin.

The receptionist's eyes widened at my utter gall, and she told me, "We address her as the mayor."

"I'm sure you do. Do me a solid and let her know I'm here, would you?" The only thing that could have made this whole scenario better was if I had gum. Can you imagine? Loudly chewing gum in a place like this? The receptionist would probably faint.

With a disdainful sniff, she picked up the phone, pressed a number, then waited. "Sorry to interrupt you, Mayor." She shot me a glare. "But Holly Day is here to see you. She doesn't have an appointment," she added. I didn't recall her asking but then figured she probably kept Kerris's diary open on her computer, and a quick glance would have told her I most certainly did not have an appointment.

"Oh?" Pause. "Okay. I'll send her through." She hung up the phone and shot me a look laced with a burning distrust. "The mayor will see you now."

I wanted to laugh. Like, really, really, laugh. But I didn't. Instead, I bit the inside of my cheek and warned my facial muscles to behave as I followed the receptionist down a hallway lined with oil painted portraits of mayors who'd served the town of

Gravestone in the past. And at the end, right before what I assumed to be Kerris's office, was Kerris's own portrait. With her dog, Jasper. "Cute." I jerked my thumb toward the painting, but the receptionist ignored me, her back ramrod straight.

"Holly Day," she announced, holding the door open for me to pass through.

"Thanks… I didn't catch your name?" My eyes swept over her, searching for a name badge, but her navy pencil skirt with matching blazer—wasn't she hot?—was pristine and revealed nothing of her identity.

"Thank you, Lydia, that will be all," Kerris decreed from behind her desk. The huge teak thing had to be the size of a king-sized bed. So big it was ridiculous. I hadn't expected anything less.

"Yeah," I called after the now retreating receptionist's back. "Thanks, Lydia."

Closing the door, I crossed to one of the two chairs strategically placed in front of Kerris's desk and took a seat. Kerris smirked, knowing I'd sat without waiting for an invitation just to annoy her. I was a trifle annoyed that she wasn't annoyed.

"You wanted to see me?" I prompted when Kerris didn't speak, merely studied me over her steepled fingers. She was a big woman. Tall, broad, overweight. The mere size of her was intimidating, and add to that her acerbic personality, and you got yourself a wholly unlikable woman. She'd rubbed me the wrong way the first time I met her, and ordinarily, I wouldn't have answered such a summons, but curiosity had gotten the better of me. I wanted to know what she wanted. And she knew it.

"I see you submitted renovation plans," she began, leaning back in her leather chair, the back squeaking as it adjusted to her weight.

"Casey did, yes. Why? If you have any technical questions, you'd best ask him. He's the builder, not me."

"So, you *are* planning on staying in Gravestone?"

I shrugged. "I have no firm plans one way or the other. But while I'm here, may as well make myself comfortable. And any renovations will only increase the value of the property." I paused. "Should I decide to sell."

"Still got that *rat*?" The way she dragged out the word rat, as if it were equal to dog poop, told me she was trying to get under my skin.

"You mean Flynn," I corrected her with a cold smile. "And yes. He's fine, thanks for asking."

"I believe you were involved in an altercation at the market on Saturday."

"What does that have to do with my building application?"

Her mouth turned down. "Nothing. Technically."

"Look, Kerris, why am I here? Time's marching on." I made an exaggerated gesture of looking at my watch, as if I had places to go, things to do.

"Gravestone Council isn't in a position to issue permits to citizens with a criminal history." She folded her arms in a *take-that* gesture.

"Good to know." I smiled, although I knew it didn't reach my eyes. In fact, I wasn't one hundred percent sure I'd pulled it off as a smile. It may have turned out more of a sneer or even a snarl. I did not like this woman, and each time I encountered her, it was hard to hide my true feelings. "Good thing I don't have a criminal record."

"You were arrested for the murder of Cody Pendant," she said triumphantly. "I'd say that counts."

"I wasn't formally arrested. The deputy put her cart before her horse and totally cocked it up, as a matter of fact. I was not read my rights. I was not processed. And I was released, with a formal apology from the sheriff. Ask him yourself if you don't believe me."

"Oh, I intend to, don't you worry."

"I'm not worried." I was starting to enjoy this. Baiting Kerris Jones was turning out to be an enjoyable pastime. Who knew? "If providing a police clearance is part of the permit application process, I'll happily oblige. In return, I want a copy of the regulations that outline that requirement. Otherwise, a person may suspect this is discrimination."

Kerris didn't say anything for several long seconds, but I saw the color flood into her face beneath the thick layer of makeup she wore, and the way her fingers gripped the edge of her desk until they turned white told me she was gathering herself, buying time while she thought of a response. It really didn't matter what Kerris Jones threw at me. I'd find a way around it. She just didn't know that yet.

"Look," I said, standing up, "you can throw all the roadblocks you want, but don't think I'll take it lying down. Reject my building permit. Fine. I'll be sure to tell everyone about our conversation today and how you're discriminating against me. I'm sure the media would love to grab hold of a story like that." No way Kerris needed to know that the last thing I needed or wanted was media attention.

"Are you threatening me?" She gasped, mouth opening in shock. I guess Kerris was so used to being the one doing the threatening that she didn't recognize it when it slapped her in the face.

"Not at all." I smiled sweetly. "Merely an observation." I turned to leave, had taken two steps when something on one of the huge floor to ceiling cabinets flanking the door caught my eye. I changed direction, veering over to it. "Well, well, well," I muttered under my breath while eyeballing the puzzle box sitting on the shelf. While not exactly the same as the one I'd bought from Macey, it was eerily similar.

"Nice puzzle box," I said, glancing at Kerris over my shoulder. She'd risen to her feet but froze when I'd approached the puzzle box. Her expression was one of panic. "Where did you get it? From Cody Pendant?"

"What?" She flapped her arms around, flustered. "I don't know. I can't remember."

"Hmmm. Interesting that *you* have a link with a murdered man."

"I don't!" she protested, voice rising, the color flaring in her cheeks.

"If you didn't get this from Cody, where did you get it?" I pressed. In all honesty, she could have picked it up from anywhere. It could have been a gift, it could have been any one of a number of things, but her reaction told me I was right—and she was most definitely hiding something, especially when she blurted, "Fine! I'll approve your permit. Now get out of my office." She pointed at the door, arm trembling.

I clasped a hand to my chest. "Why, Kerris, it's almost like you don't like me." I put on a wounded expression. "*You* were the one who invited *me* here. Now you want me to leave? All over a little puzzle box?" I tsked and shook my head. "Fine. So, I can tell Casey to expect the permit to land in his mailbox within the next few days?"

When she didn't immediately reply, I ran a finger across the top of the puzzle box, feeling the indentations.

"Yes, fine, whatever. Now go. I have another appointment."

Lifting my hand from the box, I gave her a smile and a mock salute and let myself out, closing the door with exaggerated softness behind me. If I'd thought for a minute that I'd be able to eavesdrop through the heavy thickness of the door, I would have lingered, but as it was, I couldn't hear a peep and figured, after that performance, I deserved a reward in the shape of something delicious from River's. It wouldn't hurt to apologize again and see if she'd forgiven me for the Flynn incident, either.

Sauntering out of the council offices, I gave Lydia a smile and a wave, then pulled out my phone and called Casey.

"Great news," I told him. "I just had a little chat with the mayor, and she's going to fast track the permit for us. You can expect it sometime this week."

"What? That's crazy! How did you pull that off?"

"No idea. Perhaps she likes me?"

"Our mayor doesn't like anyone. Unless she has a use for them."

I held the phone away from my ear for a second and stared at it. How unlike Casey to say something unkind about someone. He was always so warm, friendly, and, well, *kind*. But then Kerris Jones had a tendency to bring out the worse in people, so I shouldn't be surprised she'd had Matt Casey in her sights one time or another.

"Oh? Speaking from experience, Casey?"

He sighed down the phone. "Long story best kept for another day. Thanks for giving me the heads up. I'll keep an eye out for it."

CHAPTER
Eleven

It was quiet in River's, what with the Keen Agers meeting taking place and the lunch rush over. River was behind the counter and didn't look up when I entered. Rather than taking a seat, I headed straight to the counter.

"Hi, River, how's it going?"

She glanced up from where she was icing a cake. "Oh, hi, Holly. All good. You?"

"Yep, can't complain."

"Where's Doris?"

"Keen Agers meeting."

"Oooh, right." She flashed a smile. "I'd heard she was going ahead with that. Good on her. What can I get you?"

"I'll have one of those cupcakes and a cappuccino, please. And I just wanted to apologize again for Flynn's unexpected entrance yesterday. The last thing I want is for you to be in hot water with the mayor."

River returned to icing the cake, muttering, "That woman has been making my life difficult enough as it is. I'd hate to give her ammunition."

That caught my attention. Leaning my elbows on the counter, I leaned forward. "Oh? Do tell. I was just in a meeting with her. She was trying to wriggle out of approving my building permit."

Putting down the icing bag, River glanced around to make sure we wouldn't be overheard. No chance of that. I was the only customer in the café.

"Apparently, Kerris has a cousin who wants to set up shop here in Gravestone," River confided.

"And?"

"And they don't want any competition. This cousin plans on opening a bakery and wants my menu changed so I can't sell baked goods."

I barked out an astonished laugh. "They can't do that."

"Nope, they can't. But Kerris can put the pressure on. She's issuing fictitious infringement notices that result in numerous code violations that result in the health inspector being here on an almost weekly basis. He, of course, ticks off on his report that everything is fine…"

"But you don't want to give her any ammunition. I understand. And don't worry, it won't happen again. I'll talk to Flynn and explain the situation." I wondered if Doris knew about the trouble River was having with Kerris. I made a mental note to ask her.

"You'll talk to Flynn?" She paused, staring at me as if I'd lost my mind.

"Well, yeah?" I shrugged, hoping to look nonchalant, not one hundred percent sure I pulled it off. "Doesn't everyone talk to their pets? I swear he understands me. At least I think he does. He nods a lot."

River chuckled. "You're right, pretty much everyone I know who has a pet talks to it. Take a seat. I'll bring your order over shortly."

I was heading toward the table Doris and I usually sat at when something had me changing direction. Instead of choosing my usual table, I took a seat by the front window, where I had a view of the street. My sixth sense paid off, for I'd just finished the most delicious melt-in-your-mouth cupcake and was on my last mouthful of coffee when I spied Kerris Jones outside.

Not that her presence was a newsworthy event by any means, but what piqued my interest was the furtive way she was walking. She kept glancing over her shoulder as if to check if anyone was watching, head swiveling from left to right as she scurried along.

Throwing a handful of bills onto the table, I called out a farewell to River and stepped outside, following Kerris from the opposite side of the road. Making sure I kept far enough back that she wouldn't notice me and using trees as coverage, I limped after her, cursing the walking boot for the millionth time. Thankfully, she was far enough away that she didn't hear the repeated thunk as it hit the sidewalk. Given her penchant for thick tweed suits, she was easy to spot, so I was in no danger of losing sight of her. No one else in their right mind would be out walking around in this heat wearing such an outfit.

I had to hand it to her. Kerris Jones was smarter than I thought. She led me on a merry chase, and more than once, I thought she must've known I was following her as she weaved up and down and in and out of the streets with me hobbling along behind, sweating up a storm and wondering how the larger woman was coping in this weather. At one point, she stopped, opened her purse, and pulled out a handkerchief to blot her face. I'd plastered myself to the trunk of a tree, holding my breath, ignoring the sweat rolling down my face. I figured I must be bright red and dripping with perspiration by now, and it occurred to me that Kerris may be playing with me, teaching me a lesson by leading me on a wild goose chase all over town. But if that were the case, she was also putting herself at a certain level of discomfort, and I couldn't see Gravestone's mayor going to those lengths for little ol' me.

Then I hit pay-dirt. She headed down an alleyway next to an abandoned store on Wilkinson Street, its windows boarded up, the paint so faded and peeled I could no longer read the sign that had once held pride of place above the awning.

"Finally," I puffed, crossing the street to the store. Keeping close to the building, I poked my head around the corner, catching a glimpse just as Kerris reached the back of the building and stepped out of view. Voices echoed down the alley, bouncing off the walls. She was meeting someone. Someone she didn't want anyone to know about. Why else this farcical charade? And why not meet them in the comfort of her air-conditioned office? Oh, no, she was definitely up to something, and I intended to find out what.

Treading as lightly as a three-legged cat wearing a walking boot, I crept down the alley. I could make out the murmur of voices but not what they were saying. I needed to get closer. Back pressed to the wall, I peeked my head around the corner. My view was blocked by a towering stack of wooden crates. Creeping toward them, I stepped through the weeds, wincing at the overly loud crunching noise they made beneath my feet, but Kerris and her companion were too busy with their heated discussion to notice me.

Finally in position, I peered around the crates. Kerris was meeting with Dino Cittadino, and neither of them was happy.

"I'm not paying you. You didn't get the job done!" Kerris hissed, jabbing him in the chest with her finger.

"Not my fault you gave me bad intel," he shot back, mimicking her actions by jabbing her in the shoulder.

She blinked in shock that he'd dared touch her but rallied quickly. "I can end you," she spat. "Just remember that."

"You want the job done or not?" Dino drawled, seemingly unconcerned with her threat. "Because I have other clients and other jobs that pay *waaaay* better than you. You think you're some big shot wheeler and dealer? Lady, you're small fry."

She didn't like that. Her face flared red, and her eyes shot sparks while her hands clenched and unclenched. Sucking in a deep breath, she exhaled audibly, trying to regain control of her emotions.

"What happened at the market?" she asked, changing tack.

"What do you mean? Nothin' happened."

"You were seen threatening Cody Pendant. Was it you who killed him?"

Now *that* caught my interest. If Kerris had hired Dino to kill Cody, she'd hardly ask him if he was the murderer, would she? Which meant she'd hired Dino for something else entirely.

"Nah, I didn't kill him." Dino sniffed and wiped his nose on his arm. "But I had plans to rough him up later. Guess someone beat me to the punch. Anyway, no loss. The guy was a loser."

"He had his uses," she halfheartedly defended Cody.

"Yeah, that's what he wanted you to think. Truth is, your so-called artifacts? All fake. The twerp sold me a fake dagger. Me! A fake! He's got balls, I'll give him that. Only a fool would mess with the Tarkaths."

The longer I stood eavesdropping, trying not to move, the harder my foot throbbed until I could stand it no longer and had to shift my weight. Only as I adjusted my weight, I bumped the pallets. They didn't so much move as creak. But with enough volume to alert Kerris and Dino.

"What was that?" Kerris asked.

Screwing my eyes shut, I held my breath. If they spotted me, I was screwed. I had zero chance of outrunning either of them.

"Probably birds. Or rats," Dino said. "I'll check it out."

My eyes popped open. I was about to get busted big time, and with flight not an option, I'd have to settle for fight. Bending my knees, I braced myself.

"Don't bother." Kerris waved him back. "I've got to get back to the office, anyway. See that you get it done. Tonight."

"I'm gonna need the address again," Dino said, following Kerris as she started to leave.

At his words, she halted. "What?"

"I lost the address. I need it again. This is why I don't do paper."

"Well, I don't do digital. Too easy to track."

"Whatever. You want the job done or not?"

"Here." She held out her hand, palm up. "Give me your phone. I'll put the address in there so you can't lose it."

Dino handed over his phone. Kerris typed something and handed it back. "Tonight," she repeated, eyes as hard as steel.

"Guaranteed." He waited until she'd left, then turned his attention to the pallets I was hiding behind.

He took three steps toward them when his phone rang. Putting it to his ear, he answered, "Yo."

Yo? The guy had to be sixty if he was a day and he answered with yo? He listened to whoever was on the other end of the line, one hand stroking his beard. His attention was on the ground, where he was scuffing the dirt with his boot.

"Yep. Uh-huh. Okay. Is the intel good?" He paused, shuffled around a bit, then turned his back to me. I let out a shuddering breath I hadn't realized I'd been holding.

"The mayor's working with us. Unless she's thinking of double-crossing—" Whoever he was talking to cut him off, and he paused to listen. "Got it." Hanging up, he headed off down the driveway, whistling as he went. I waited a full five minutes before I slowly followed, creeping down the alley. At the end, I poked my head around, searched one way, then the other. Dino and Kerris were both long gone, but who should I see heading straight for me?

"Holly?" Calder lowered his sunglasses, peering over them as if to check his eyes weren't playing tricks on him. "What are you doing here?"

I glanced at the dilapidated old store behind me. "Just exploring the town. I guess this place hasn't been open in a while?"

He glanced at the store, then back at me. "It's an old electrical store. Owner retired. Most folks travel into Corpus Christi for their needs these days."

"Right." I nodded, shuffled my feet, winced, and did

my best to ignore the trickle of sweat running between my shoulder blades. It was as hot as Hades, and I'd come out without a hat or water. I could feel the heat in my face, knew I must be burned, and was reasonably certain I was a sight to behold. After another moment's silence, Calder confirmed it.

"You look a tad overheated. Dare I offer you a lift, or will you bite my head off?"

If my face could get any hotter, it would. He was referring to my arrival in Gravestone, when he'd picked me up from where Hector, the bus driver, had dropped me, and I'd been less than grateful. In my defense, I was hot, in pain, and had come to the bone crushing realization that the walk into town was miles. Plus, being benched by the SIA still rankled. It hadn't been my best moment.

I looked behind him. No sheriff's truck in sight. "With what?" I asked. "You walked here."

"Station's just around the corner." He jerked his thumb. "Had a report of a disturbance at the old store and figured I'd walk by to check it out."

"A disturbance?" I glanced up and down the deserted street. No one was about. Everyone had the good sense to stay inside during the hottest part of the day. Except for me, of course. I had to give Kerris credit. It was a pretty good plan of hers, meeting up with Dino when everyone was behind closed doors enjoying their AC.

"Phil Harmonic lives across the street." Calder jerked his head toward the tiny house with a massive palm tree out front. "Called to say he saw some folks around the store. Thought they were up to no good."

I knew what was coming, and Calder didn't disappoint. With a cocky smirk, he added, "Shoulda known it was only you."

"Har har." I executed a mock bow. "Very funny. But yes, thank you, if the offer for a lift is still open?" I leaned against the side of the building to take the weight off my now throbbing foot. Foolish mistake to walk all over town with an injury. Calder's eyes ran over me, coming to rest on my foot with its strapped on, cumbersome boot, then swinging back up to my face. What I saw in his eyes had my heart doing that weird thing again. Jumping in my chest and then galloping away, thundering as if I were running a marathon, making it hard to breathe.

"You're in pain. Wait here, I'll get the truck." He spun on his heel and strode back the way he'd come, long legs eating up the sidewalk, denim hugging his rear, catching my attention. I watched until he was out of sight, then shook my head. "Get it together Twitch," I whispered. "A dalliance with the local sheriff is a really bad idea." Yeah, tell my libido that!

Less than a minute later, Calder was back, truck pulling up to the curb, engine idling. Hobbling across the sidewalk, I opened the passenger door and climbed in, trying not to wince and probably failing, judging by the concerned look on his face.

"Who were you following?" he asked, pulling away as soon as I'd clicked the seatbelt into place.

"What?"

"Phil's report said he saw folks around the store. Plural. As in more than one."

"I know what plural means."

"I turn up and who do I find? You. You, with a fractured foot. And please don't tell me you were sightseeing. I'm not buying it, so you may as well save us both some time and tell me the truth."

I did all the things I'd look for in a suspect. I sucked in a breath, I chewed my lip, I kept my gaze out the window, refusing to look at him. And I caved. "I saw Kerris Jones having a clandestine meeting with Dino Cittadino."

"Where? At the store?" He didn't sound surprised.

I nodded. "Behind the store. I assume it used to be a parking lot? But yes, I was at River's when I saw the mayor acting... furtive. It piqued my curiosity, so I followed her."

"The old store is like two minutes from the foreshore, yet the state you're in, you look like you walked miles."

It was so kind of him to point that out. "Because I did. Kerris led me on a merry chase. She weaved in and around the streets for a good half hour before arriving here."

"So, she knew you were following her?"

I shook my head. "Actually, no, I don't think she did. She wouldn't have gone ahead with meeting Dino if she'd known. I think the whole charade was *in case* someone was following her. She didn't know someone actually was."

"We'll come back to why you were following the mayor." Calder tapped his fingers on the steering wheel. "Did you overhear what they were saying?"

Adjusting the vents to direct cool air onto my overheated skin, I grinned. "Of course. Kerris has hired Dino to do something, and whatever it is, it's going down tonight."

"Do you know what that something is?"

"Sadly, no. Kerris was fuming because apparently Dino was supposed to have done the job already, but he lost the address. She'd written it down for him, but he lost it." And that's when the pieces of the puzzle fell into place. Clutching Calder's arm, momentarily distracted by the firm muscles beneath my touch, I blurted, "I think the address Kerris wrote and Dino lost? It was mine. It was my name and address you found in Cody's cold, dead hand."

Twelve

Calder pulled up outside my house, keeping the engine running. "I'll get a sample of the mayor's handwriting, do a comparison analysis."

"There's something else," I added, unbuckling my seatbelt. "Dino said Cody had sold him a fake dagger. They got into it at the market. Dino was furious, but Kerris asked Dino outright if he killed Cody, and Dino said no."

"He could have lied," Calder pointed out.

"Yeah, he could have. But I don't think he did. I don't think Dino killed Cody. Anyway, thanks for the ride." I opened the door, but Calder grabbed my arm before I could slide out.

"Holly? Be careful, okay? If it's true that your name was on that scrap of paper because you're the job the mayor hired Dino for, then Dino is coming for you."

I couldn't help the grin that slid across my face. I

lived for moments like this, the adrenaline rush, the thrill of the chase. "Let him come. I'm not afraid."

"I know you're not, and that's what scares me."

"Relax." I laid my hand over his where it still gripped my arm, his touch doing strange things to my insides. "I'm a trained professional." And then I slapped a hand over my mouth because I'd never meant to reveal that. With huge eyes, I stared at him, begging him not to call me on it. Not to probe, not to pry for the truth.

He didn't answer immediately. Instead, I got lost in his hazel eyes, mesmerized by the specks of gold and the dark, swirling depths dragging me in and sucking me under. So, when he said, "Your secret is safe with me," it took me a red hot second to understand what he was talking about.

He loosened his grip, and I slid out of the car. Standing in the open door, I looked at him. "You don't need to worry about me." I did my best to reassure him. "Because I don't think Dino is out to kill me."

His brows shot up. "You don't?"

"Nope. I think all of this," I waved my hand around, "has to do with the puzzle box and what it contains. I think Kerris got wind that I had it, and she wants Dino to steal it from me. That's why my name and address are on that scrap of paper."

"But someone did break into your house," he pointed out.

"It wasn't Dino. The build was all wrong. It was someone slimmer. And, as yet, we don't know what that person was after. They were upstairs going through the bookcase."

"Are you saying you don't think they were after the puzzle box?" His tone told me he didn't believe it for one second, and I had to admit, he was most likely right.

I shrugged. "They probably were," I admitted. "Whoever it was wasn't aware that I've been sleeping in the living room—they assumed I'd be upstairs in my bedroom and that I'd probably taken the box with me." The intruder had made all sorts of assumptions, all of them wrong.

"It's all guesswork at this stage," he agreed. He ran his eyes over me again. The trail they took heated my blood, my pulse pounded in my throat. "Rest up. I'll check on you later."

"I don't need anyone to check up on me," I automatically protested.

"I know you don't. Just humor me, okay?"

Surprising us both, I said, "Okay," then slammed the door shut and made my way down the cracked and weed strewn front path. Calder waited until I was inside and the door shut before he drove away. Closing my eyes, I leaned back against the front door. "Oh boy," I whispered. "I think I'm in trouble."

Squeak?

"It's okay," I reassured Flynn. "I'm fine."

A barrage of squeaks followed, complete with paw waving. I figured Flynn did not agree that I was okay.

"I'm going to take a shower, and then I'll fill you in,

okay?" Flynn followed me upstairs, stopping short of following me into the bathroom only when I stopped and turned to face him. "Really? We're having this conversation? Again?" If a rat's face could look sullen, Flynn pulled it off. With his little feet stomping in what I could only imagine to be a fit of pique, he stomped his way to the top of the staircase, but rather than going back downstairs and waiting for me in the air-conditioned bliss of the living room, he sat on the top stair, settling in for the wait.

"Fine." I threw up my hands. "Sit there and wait. Honestly, you men are impossible. I'm totally fine, and I'm more than capable of taking a shower without keeling over."

But the sight that greeted me when I looked at myself in the mirror in the bathroom had me widening my eyes in horror. I was tomato red. And my hair hung in lank strands where it had escaped my ponytail but was literally soaked with sweat. No wonder I felt like a train wreck because I most certainly looked one. What was I thinking, running around outside at the hottest part of the day with no protection? "I'm a trained agent," I whispered to myself. "I know better. I can do better." But there was no denying I'd been off my game ever since uncovering the counterfeit wands. The sooner Harding gave me the all-clear to return to work, the better. I needed to get back out in the field and hone my rapidly declining skills.

Stripping out of yet another set of sweat-soaked clothes, I stepped beneath the shower, wincing when the water hit my sunburned skin. Maybe Doris had some sort of salve that would take the sting out? I'd message her as soon as I was done. I needed to bring her up to speed, anyway.

I was down to my last pair of shorts and my second to last tank top. The remainder of my clothes were in a dirty pile on the floor, waiting to be washed. Which meant either buying a washing machine or visiting a laundromat, and despite my exploration of Gravestone today, I didn't recall passing a laundromat.

Giving my walking boot yet another wipe down, I carried it with me downstairs, propping it against the bottom of the staircase to dry. Popping a couple of pain killers, I fired up the coffee pot and messaged Doris.

> What do you have for sunburn?

> Keen Agers went brilliantly

> That's fantastic. So happy for you.

> Are you being sarcastic?

> No. I'm genuinely pleased. But also sunburned. Do you have a salve?

> I'll be right over.

I assumed that meant she did. While I waited for her to turn up, I fixed myself a coffee and took a seat in the camp chair, my foot resting on the cot, while Flynn sat on the arm of my chair, indicating with a wave of his paw that he was waiting for an explanation. I'd just finished regaling him with the afternoon's pursuits when I heard the Impala out front.

"Come in," I yelled before Doris had a chance to knock.

"Phew, much better in here." Doris slammed the front door behind her, and the whole house shook. If Casey hadn't assured me the foundation was sound, I'd be worried about the whole abode collapsing like a house of cards. "You weren't kidding when you said you had a sunburn." She bent to examine my face. "You're as red as a beet. Does it hurt?" She poked my cheek, making me wince.

"Yes," I snapped, jerking away. "It does hurt."

"Here. This'll fix you right up." Rummaging in her oversize purse, she pulled out a jar with a red lid and no label. "Rub this on. It'll leave a greasy residue, but it soothes the burn and will take the redness right out."

Unscrewing the lid, I peered at the balm inside. It was blue. And I'm not talking an attractive amethyst shade of blue. No, this blue was a dark navy. Emphasis on the dark. "It's not going to take the redness out by turning my skin blue, is it?" I asked suspiciously.

Doris grinned. "No." Was she lying? I couldn't tell. Seeing my hesitation, she stuck her fingers into the jar and rubbed the salve onto the back of her hand. We both watched as the blue faded, leaving nothing but a glowing shine on her skin.

"Okay then." Satisfied, I dipped my fingers in and

rubbed the salve over my face, neck, and shoulders. The relief was immediate, and I sighed.

"Better?"

"Much. Coffee?" I made a move to get up, but Doris waved me back into my seat.

"I'll get it. You're resting with your foot up, which means you probably overdid it today and now that broken bone of yours is throbbing like a son-of-a-beach. Stay put, and I'll get the coffee."

"I think you know me a little too well," I teased, admitting defeat. "Tell me about the inaugural Keen Agers meeting."

Heading into the kitchen, Doris called over her shoulder, "It was great! All the old crew turned up, except those in allegiance with Kerris. It was just like old times."

"Who was there?"

"Bernadette Bridge, Vera Cherrington, Carmella Highwater, Ethel Dawes, Gladys Overwith, Valda Collins, Ophelia Paine, and the two Ada's; Ada Rose Bartlett and Ada Florence Holmes."

"Quite the turnout." And if my memory served me, it was the same crew who'd turned up and helped clean John Smith's house when I first arrived. The only person missing was Denise Hurt.

"Enough about me. What were you up to this afternoon that saw you get burned to a crisp?" She came back cradling a cup of coffee and made herself comfortable on the cot.

I repeated what I'd already told Flynn, that the

meeting with Kerris had gone better than expected, and I'd secured the building permit, the puzzle box that looked like mine, and the fact that she'd snuck out to meet with Dino Cittadino shortly after I'd left. When I revealed that Calder and I thought the scrap of paper with my name and address had been written by Kerris and given to Dino, who'd subsequently lost it, and that the job Kerris had hired him for was going down tonight, she jumped to the same conclusion we did.

"She hired him to break in here." Doris looked at me, concerned. "Was it him last night?"

I shook my head. "No, like I told Calder, the build was wrong, and it couldn't have been Dino because he'd lost my address. Probably hadn't even looked at the scrap of paper when Kerris gave it to him, just shoved it into his pocket, figuring he'd read it later, when he was ready to do the job." It did make me slightly uneasy that the *job* was me. What were Kerris's intentions? Did she want me killed? Or was it something within these walls that she was after? I was coming to the realization that there was more to John Smith than anyone in Gravestone realized, and now that word of his demise had gotten around, the vultures were swarming.

"I can't help but think that Dino is here because of the hit on me," I confessed, twisting my cup in my hands. "It's the only thing that makes sense." It was the one thing I hadn't told Calder. My secret identity. The price on my head. Only I didn't know who was coming for me—the Tarkaths or the Arzans, or someone else entirely. But they were coming, I was sure of it.

Doris looked disbelieving. "You think Kerris Jones knows who you are for real? And that there's a hit on you from some mobster peddling counterfeit wands and Kerris knows and she's tipped Dino off, so she can what? Claim the bounty?"

I chewed my lip. "When you put it that way…"

Doris ignored me. "There's no way Kerris knows any of that, or she'd have had Calder arrest you as soon as you set foot in town. I don't think she has a clue as to your real identity—but she definitely either wants this house or something in it."

"The puzzle box? But I only bought it at the market on Saturday. How could she know I've got it?"

"Hon, the whole town knows you bought it from Cody Pendant's stall and the massive tantrum he threw when he realized you had it. I would say that's what Kerris has hired Dino for. To get the box."

I relaxed a little at the thought Kerris was after the puzzle box, not me. "But she doesn't know we got it open."

Doris froze, mouth agape. "You got it open, and you didn't tell me?" She leaned over and punched my arm, hard.

"Ow!" Flinching, I rubbed my now dead arm. The woman was a menace.

"Spill. What was inside? Where is it? Show me!"

"Okay, okay, calm down. Sorry, it was an oversight on my behalf. I wasn't intentionally keeping it from you, but there's been a lot going on." I strapped my boot back on before heaving myself out of the chair. "What do you know about soul stones?" I asked, heading upstairs. I'd ingeniously hidden the crystal in the bathroom, wedged between a shampoo bottle and a loofa.

"Soul stones are pretty rare." Doris shouted to be heard over my footfalls on the stairs, lowering her voice when I appeared in the doorway holding the crystal. "Oh, my stars." She reached for the crystal, and I handed it to her, watching as she turned it over and over in her hands. "This could be very bad for Gravestone."

I nodded, resuming my seat. "That's what I figured, too. Could it destroy the ley line?"

She nodded. "Potentially? Yes. So this is what Keelan Moore paid Cody to procure for him."

"Uh-huh."

"And yet it is Dino Cittadino who has you in his cross-hairs."

"Strikes me as odd too," I agreed. Aside from Keelan's single approach to get me to give him the puzzle box, I hadn't heard anything more from the man. A cold rush wrapped around me, causing goosebumps to pimple my skin and a shiver to shoot up my spine. He wouldn't have given up, not that easily. It would be foolish of me to think he had. Maybe he knew of Dino's involvement and was waiting for me to be distracted by whatever Dino had planned before he struck. Maybe he and Dino were working together?

"Did you feel that?" I whispered to Doris. Her wide eyes met mine.

"Something ominous?" she whispered back. I nodded. She tossed the soul stone at me with no warning. I flung myself back to catch it, only my momentum caused the chair to topple backward, and soon, I was flat on my back, staring up at the ceiling, the breath knocked from my lungs.

"What'd'cha do that for?" I wheezed.

"I don't want to touch the damn thing." Doris rubbed her hands on her thighs as if wiping away any residual energy from the stone.

"What do we do with it? Put it back in the puzzle box?" Clambering out of the chair, I righted it and resumed my seat, the stone in my left hand.

"No. Too obvious. Way too many people know the stone is in the box. We're going to have to hide it somewhere else until we can get rid of it."

"Where?"

Then we said in unison, "The cedar elm tree."

CHAPTER
Thirteen

"**P**lease be careful," I called, standing beneath the cedar elm and looking up into the branches. I couldn't see Doris or Flynn, which was the whole point. We'd figured this to be the best hiding spot when Seth Saltzman's bones had turned up, and it would do equally well as a hiding spot for the soul stone. The only problem was I couldn't climb the tree thanks to my stupid broken foot, so Doris had to, and despite watching her shimmy up the massive tree twice now, my heart still stuttered in my chest at the sight of a senior citizen climbing a tree.

"Ye of little faith," Doris shot back over the sound of duct tape ripping from the roll, only for her to curse and say "oops" seconds before the duct tape came plummeting to earth, narrowly missing me.

"Doris!" I scolded.

"Sorry! But the good news is we're all done. Thanks, Flynn."

Flynn came scrambling down with a knife clutched between his teeth, followed by Doris.

"Now we hide the puzzle box inside." She clapped me on the shoulder, and I staggered. "Let them think that once they find it, they've got the prize."

"My thoughts exactly."

We hid the puzzle box in the freezer behind a packet of frozen peas. I didn't remember buying peas and wondered where they'd come from. Maybe Doris had put them there? Or one of the Keen Agers on our cleaning bee. But they definitely didn't belong to John Smith because I recalled cleaning out the fridge and freezer.

"The lining of the freezer should help hide any residual magic the box contains," Doris said, hands on hips, admiring her handiwork.

"Magic? Is the soul stone emitting magic?" I hadn't thought of that. If it was, then hiding it in the tree was a waste of time. It would be a beacon to all and sundry. "Wouldn't the fact that it's in Gravestone, which hides magic, negate that?"

"Yes and no," she said cryptically. "But don't worry, I put it in a cloth bag before taping it to the branch."

"A bag?"

"A *cloth* bag."

"Right. Because that makes all the difference."

"It does if it's charmed." She winked, then grabbed her purse. "I'm off. Promised Gladys I'd watch *Dirty Dancing* with her on the VCR tonight. If you're still alive in the morning, we'll finish sorting out this bookcase."

She pointed toward the bookcase in question, half-empty with some books packed in boxes, others strewn on the floor, then gave me a quick wave and slipped out the door with her customary slam.

"If I'm still alive," I sniggered. "They have no idea who they're dealing with." Grabbing a fresh bag of salt from the kitchen, I opened the front door, assessing the damage Doris's slamming had done to the ward I'd laid down. Yep. As suspected, half of it was blown away. Laying down a new trail, I carefully closed the door so as not to disturb it, then grabbed the sage Doris had brought with her and lit it, wafting the smoke throughout the house, not so much to deter demons, but to cleanse any lingering magic the soul stone may have left behind.

With the house freshly warded and cleansed, I got busy in the kitchen, baking another loaf of bread.

"You know," I said to Flynn, who was sitting on the sink watching the proceedings, "I should approach River, see if she'd be interested in buying some of this bread off me, because if I keep baking at this rate, the two of us are going to resemble a loaf of bread with the weight we put on."

Flynn squeaked and nodded, which I took to mean he thought it was a good idea. While the dough was rising, I cleaned up, then kneaded the dough one final time before scooping it into a pan and sliding it into the oven. The extra heat from the oven made the kitchen even hotter, but it was a sacrifice I was prepared to make. And only a short one at that. Once the renovations were done, I'd have air-conditioning. As it was, I'd left the door that separated the kitchen from the living room open, allowing some of the cool air to drift through.

Then I heard it. The creaking of a floorboard overhead. I looked at Flynn, who was standing on his haunches, nose lifted to the ceiling, sniffing.

"Shh," I whispered, finger to my lips. He looked at me, gave a nod, then scampered across the sink, leaping to the floor before running up the stairs. This was it. Dino was here. But how had he gotten in? I glanced at my watch. It was only just past eight o'clock. I hadn't expected him so early, but maybe he was a busy thug, and I wasn't the only one on his agenda this evening.

Bending, I undid the straps of my walking boot as quietly as I could, the ripping of the Velcro sounding unbelievably loud in the silence. I could hear the ticking of the timer on the oven, the sound of my own breaths, and nothing else. The creaking of the floorboards upstairs had stopped. Did that mean Dino was on the staircase? Or already downstairs? For a big man, he trod very lightly.

Creeping across the floor, I kept my back to the wall while I peeked through the open doorway. The lamp was on in the living room, throwing a soft yellow light across the room, but of Dino, there was no sign. I turned my attention to the staircase, shrouded in darkness. Rolling my shoulders, I straightened my spine and began the journey up. My eyes were adjusting to the darkness and so far, no sign of Dino Cittadino.

On the landing, I paused to listen. I thought I heard a sound coming from the front bedroom and turned in that direction when a figure suddenly appeared in the open doorway. Even though I was expecting it, I still gasped, my heart skipping a beat and goosebumps puckering my skin.

I decided to attack rather than waiting to be attacked. With a yell, I launched myself at Dino. Only he danced backward, remarkably light on his feet for a man of his size. Then the bedroom light flickered on, which was confusing because if Dino was in front of me, and the light switch was behind me, who had turned it on? It couldn't have been Flynn. There was no furniture in the room for him to climb to reach the switch.

"Oh." It was not Dino Cittadino standing in front of me. Under the light of the single bulb swinging from the ceiling stood Claire Whelan. Which meant her husband Beau had to be behind me. A quick glance over my shoulder confirmed it. I'd been prepared to battle with one very big thug but two demons? I'd manage. Bending my knees, I relaxed my body, shook out my shoulders, and braced myself for whatever they were about to throw at me.

"I'm so sorry!" Claire cried. "We didn't mean to scare you."

Okay. Not what I thought she was going to say, but then they could be trying to lull me into a false sense of security. I didn't say a word but remained vigilant. I daren't take my eyes off her and search for Flynn. Why hadn't he come downstairs to warn me it wasn't Dino, that demons had gained entry? Which got me thinking, how had they gained entry? I'd warded the house, I'd laid down fresh salt, and yet…

My eyes darted to the window. The open window, where the trail of salt had been disturbed. And there was Flynn, sitting on the sill, examining the salt trail. I wanted to slap myself in the head. Of course. We'd been up here packing up the books. And Doris had closed the window. Or, more accurately, slammed the window, creating enough of a gust of wind to dislodge the salt. Only I hadn't thought to check up here. I hadn't checked any of the upstairs windows, assuming them to be intact. Rookie error on my part.

"We're not here to cause trouble." Beau joined his wife, placing an arm around her waist in a show of solidarity and affection.

I blinked, not sure what to make of this turn of events. I relaxed my fighting stance a fraction. If they were here to kill me, they'd have done so already. They wouldn't be standing around chatting first.

"Why not knock?" I asked. "You know, at the front door. Like normal people."

"We were worried you'd slam the door in our faces," Claire said, wringing her hands together. "And we really wanted a chance to explain."

"We know you were at our house," Beau cut in. "Claire saw you."

Guess I couldn't very well complain that they'd

broken into my house when Doris and I had broken into theirs first. Turnabout was fair play, after all.

"We know that you know," Beau continued.

"That we're demons," Claire added.

I nodded once. "Right."

"Hence the salting, am I right?" Beau glanced at the windowsill and the remnants of salt.

"Correct." No point in denying it. "So you're here now. Spill. What's so important you felt the need to break the wards and enter my home?"

Beau bristled at that, his brows pulling low, his fingers digging into Claire's hip. "That's rich coming from you. You were snooping on private property."

"Babe, shhh." Claire turned to her husband, cupped his face in her palms, pulling his attention to her. "It'll be okay. Let me explain to her, okay? Like we agreed."

He rested his forehead against hers and closed his eyes, pulled in a deep breath before slowly releasing it. I got it. Claire centered him. Grounded him. It was sweet, and on one level, I kinda envied the connection they had. On the other hand, I had two demons who'd just gained entry to my home.

Claire turned her attention back to me. "You must know by now that Gravestone is special, yes? That it has unique, mystical abilities?"

I nodded.

"We came here like many others, seeking a new life. You see, we escaped Purgatory. We're refugees. We just wanted to get married, raise a family, have a normal life. We're not hurting anyone and don't intend to."

"You escaped Purgatory?" My eyebrows shot into my hairline.

She nodded. "With a little help." She glanced around the room we were standing in, a sad expression on her face. "All we ask is that you keep our secret. The fewer people who know our true identities, the better."

I'd be all kinds of hypocritical if I denied their request. After all, I was in Gravestone under false pretenses and in hiding myself. Who was I to blow their cover? Unless, of course, they were murderers.

"Did you kill Cody Pendant?"

They shook their heads in unison. "No. We did not. We were angry at him, sure. We paid over two thousand dollars for that antique dresser. Only when we got it home, we discovered the *Made in China* sticker on the bottom. A little research told us that the dresser retailed online for around six hundred dollars. We just wanted the difference back—we still love the dresser, but it sure isn't worth what we paid for it."

"Plus, bashing his head in isn't our style," Beau grumbled, eyes flashing red for the briefest of moments. "If we'd done it, you'd have never found the body."

I sighed. "Yeah, that's what I figured." A demon would have a way of making a body disappear. They'd never be so sloppy as to leave the victim where they would be found. "Okay, fine. I won't out you."

Claire beamed, rushing forward to wrap me in a hug. "Thank you so much, Holly."

"I'm sorry we snooped around your place," I

surprised myself by saying. What the hell was wrong with me? I never apologized for doing my job!

"That's okay. We understand why you did. You were just trying to clear your name, and we did argue with Cody at the market, so…" She shrugged. "I guess we should go." She turned toward the window.

"Why don't you use the front door, hmm?" I suggested.

"No need," Beau assured me, then, clasping his wife's hand, they both stepped through the window and disappeared. It was fascinating and spooky as hell.

"Well!" I said to Flynn, who was still sitting motionless on the windowsill. "That was a bit of excitement, eh? You okay?"

He shook himself out of the stupor he was in, a full-on body shake, then leaped from the windowsill and ran out of the room. I stood at the window, peering into the night. No sign of the Whelans, but then, I hadn't expected any. Maybe they had some sort of portal system. Maybe they flew. I didn't know, but I did know they didn't travel here under conventional methods. Closing the window, I eyeballed the messed-up line of salt. Should I lay more salt, or could I relax, having cleared the air with the Whelans? Deciding I'd err on the side of caution, I made my way downstairs, put my walking boot back on, and grabbed the open box of salt before returning upstairs to lay a fresh trail across the windowsill. "Just as a precaution," I told myself. Maybe the Whelans weren't the only demons in town.

Fourteen

"You have got to be kidding me!" I hissed to Flynn hours later when I was woken by the sound of floorboards creaking overhead. I'd closed the window. I'd laid down fresh salt. Which told me it wasn't the Whelans popping back in for another visit. It had to be Dino Cittadino doing the job Kerris had hired him to do.

The rattling of the AC covered any noises I made as I eased myself off the cot. My walking boot lay on the floor next to the bed, and I left it there. Easier to sneak around without it. An uneasy feeling slithered up my spine, making the hairs on my nape stand on end.

"Stay out of the way," I whispered to Flynn. "I don't want you hurt. And if this goes bad, go get Calder, okay?" Through the dimness of the night, I thought I saw him nod.

Creeping up the stairs, I paused, listening. Nothing. A feeling of déjà vu swept over me. This was just like earlier, when the Whelans had paid a visit. Floorboards creaking, then silence. I eased myself up the final step and onto the landing, had just reached the doorway, back plastered to the wall, when a hand reached around, grabbed my shirt, and hiked me into the room.

I yelped. Dino Cittadino had my T-shirt in his fist and a smirk on his face, and I appreciated neither. That he'd gotten the jump on me was incredibly annoying. Without so much as a second thought, I reared my head back and head-butted him, the crack my forehead made against his nose supremely satisfying. He cursed, easing his grip, and I slipped out of his hold, darting behind him to deliver a kick to the back of his knee. He went down like a ton of bricks, the house shuddering at the impact.

"Why you little—" he ground out, springing to his feet and turning to face me. Blood dripped from his nose, over his chin, and into his beard.

I grunted as I took a blow from Dino. Only it wasn't a blow, it was like a push of power erupted from Dino's fist. Who brought magic to a fistfight? An underhanded scoundrel like Dino Cittadino, I guess. Silly me to think he'd fight with honor. And sillier me not to think of bringing a weapon with me.

"You don't know who you're dealing with, do you, little witch?" he said, with a soft venom that did nothing to make him less scary. Waves of power crashed over me that made me catch my breath as though I were being dunked in a bath of hot, then cold water. My skin prickled and danced with the power of it.

The gloves were off. There was no way I could fight his magic without my own and win. Throwing caution to the wind, I unfurled my fingers, felt my magic roll up through my body, ready to release. I flung my hand toward him, expecting him to recoil from the blow. But nothing happened. No magical blast. Not even a minuscule pop. *What the hell?* Harding had warned me against using magic, but had he hexed me so I *couldn't?* No time to think about it now with Dino breathing down my neck. I had no choice but to fight him unaided, with nothing but my fists and wit.

"How about you quit hiding behind magic and fight me like a real man?" I taunted. "Or don't you have the balls?" I allowed my gaze to travel the length of him, my expression telling him I didn't think he was up to the job.

He rose to the challenge like I'd hoped, lunging for me while I danced out of the way. I may be smaller, but I was faster. And smarter. Only my broken foot was my Achilles heel, allowing Dino to land more blows than I'd have liked.

"Why did you kill Cody?" We were circling each other, breathless, searching for weakness in our opponent.

"What? I didn't kill that weasel. Why would I?"

"Duh! Because he ripped you off! Sold you a fake dagger." I needed to get him talking and figured the best way was to accuse him of a murder I knew he didn't commit.

His eyes narrowed. "How did you know about that?"

"Doesn't matter how I know, I just know. If you didn't kill Cody, who did?"

"Don't know and don't care, but it wasn't me. Anyway, I have an alibi."

"Sure you do."

"I do! I was with the mayor."

"You were with the mayor. Doing what?" The grin that flashed across his face told me all I needed to know. "Gross. That's so gross." Dino landed a punch that had me seeing double.

Heaving for breath and hurting in places I'd forgotten could hurt, I blinked through the stars blurring my vision. This was not how it would end. I would not go out this way, taken down by some Tarkath gangster who should have been pulling a pension rather than punches.

Dino roared and charged like a bull, head down, arms out wide. His head collided with my abdomen, knocking what little breath I had left clean out of me, and we flew backward onto the landing, then down. Head over heels, we tumbled in a tangle of limbs and curses down the staircase. How neither of us snapped our necks, I don't know, but we landed with a bone crushing crash at the foot of the stairs.

"Ow," I groaned, spitting out a mouthful of blood.

"Had enough, witch?"

I figured he meant to sound menacing, but it was hard to take him seriously with the wheezing breaths peppering his words.

"Have you?" I crawled away, using the wall to pull myself upright, taking a minute to catch my breath.

Dino laughed, then coughed before dragging himself to his feet. He turned to me as I swung a right hook, using what little energy I had left. I caught him in the side of the head, right in the temple. I turned and bolted but wasn't fast enough. Dino charged, plowing me into the living room wall. To my—and I suspect his —utter surprise, we crashed right through the wall separating the living room from the kitchen, plaster and debris raining over us, splinters of wood digging into my back as I lay on the kitchen floor staring up at the ceiling, wondering if Casey would be annoyed I'd started demolition without him.

I rolled to my belly, not feeling anything but pure adrenaline as I crawled toward the back door. A hand clamped on my ankle, and I shook Dino off with a kick to his face.

I was scrambling away, clawing at the floor, trying to gain purchase, when the whole house shuddered, and the front door crashed in. I was expecting to see Calder. Instead, a great big black bear bounded into the house, stood on his back legs, his head brushing the ceiling, and roared. Loud enough that the windows rattled. Loud enough that I just may have peed my pants a little.

I was at the back door, fiddling with the bolt, my

fumbling fingers next to useless, when Dino caught up with me, grabbed me by the upper arms and swung me around, using me as a shield between him and the bear. I screwed my eyes shut and kissed my butt goodbye as the bear approached with thundering steps, claws glistening in the moonlight streaming through the front door, crunching over the debris from the impromptu kitchen renovation.

"Argh!" I screamed as Dino literally threw me at the bear. Arms and legs waving, I flew through the air, landed against the beast, and had a brief moment to wonder at how soft its fur was. Like, really soft. Like a kitten. Like Flynn's. Then the bear's front legs wrapped around me, and I knew this was it. I was about to die, crushed to death by a bear in my kitchen. As you do.

Only the arms didn't squeeze the breath from my body. Instead, they gently cradled me, swept me in a semi-circle to deposit me behind it before turning back to Dino. And then the bear roared again, and I covered my ears, for this roar was full of pissed-offed-ness rage.

Dino quit fiddling with the bolt, snatched a knife from the sink—why hadn't I thought of that?—and spun on his heels, throwing the knife. End over end, it flashed past the bear—who jerked out of the way— before burying itself into my right shoulder. I bellowed and went down.

Dino gave up trying to unlock the door and instead kicked it down, his own panic at being eviscerated lending him extra strength. He leaped through the opening, taking off at the speed of light into the night. The bear followed as far as the back porch before stopping, lowering to all fours, and watching the fleeing villain.

My shoulder stung like the devil, and I eyeballed the blade sticking out. I suspected adrenaline was dulling the pain somewhat, but I was wary of pulling it out in case I bled to death there on my living room floor. Plus, the bear was still around. I wasn't safe yet.

I briefly considered crawling my sorry ass upstairs and hiding out in one of the bedrooms but figured if the bear had smashed in the front door with little effort, a flimsy bedroom door wasn't going to keep it out. Flynn came skidding in through the front doorway, saw me on the ground, and immediately climbed onto my chest, his head swiveling from the knife in my shoulder to my face.

"Flynn," I wheezed. "Run, buddy. There's a bear. You'd make a tasty hors d'oeuvre', and I really don't think I could take the guilt if he ate you."

But Flynn was shaking his head and doing this whole sign language thing that I didn't understand, and my head was swimming. "Go, go," I begged. "Before it comes back." For it had to come back, didn't it? Only… it was taking its sweet time. Several minutes had passed since it had chased Dino out the back door. Maybe it had followed the gangster after all?

"Holly? You okay?"

Standing where the living room doorway used to be

was Sheriff Joshua Calder, buck naked except for one of my tea towels strategically held across his hips. I was embarrassingly slow on the uptake. Blame it on one-too-many punches to the head courtesy of Dino, because I did not immediately put two and two together. "Calder! Run. Get your gun. There's a bear." Followed two seconds later by, "Why aren't you wearing any clothes?"

He grinned, but I barely noticed because my eyes had drifted to his naked chest, devouring the hills and valleys of his muscled torso, abdomen, and thighs.

"Holly," he said, his deep, sexy voice all deep and, well, sexy. "You may regret looking at me like that."

My gaze bounced back up to his face. It didn't help. "Doubtful." I slapped a hand to my face at the corny line, then winced when the movement reminded me of the knife buried to the hilt in my shoulder. It barely registered over the lust currently flooding my bloodstream, and I had to wonder if I wasn't under the influence of some sort of spell. How could I, after being in a brawl with a gangster, with a blade protruding from my body, be eying Calder with what could only be described as lust?

His full mouth showed traces of a smile that reached all the way up to his sparkling hazel eyes, the green and gold flecks brilliant in the dim light. A deep hunger flashed in his irises. It caused heat to flood my abdomen, and my cheeks flamed.

I felt a warmth, a rush of fire and heat; then I felt a

mouth at my ear and heard a voice so deep, so husky, the low vibration curled over me in sensual waves. "How about we remove that blade, hmmm?"

Jolted out of my carnal fantasy, I glanced down at my shoulder. Yes. Right. Remove the knife. Good idea.

Flynn ran to the kitchen, retrieved another tea towel, and returned, dragging it across the debris-strewn floor to deposit it on my lap.

"Thanks, Flynn, but I think I may need something a little more… hygienic."

Calder glanced at the tea towel Flynn had just dragged across the floor. "She's right, mate. Hold tight while I go grab a towel."

My eyes just about bugged out of my head when Calder turned and headed up the stairs, giving me an unobstructed view of his bare butt. "Holy cheese crackers," I whispered, closing my eyes. Flynn remained sitting on my thigh while I lay prone on the floor. The image of Calder's naked body burned in my mind. I listened as he moved about upstairs. Seconds later, he returned, this time with a towel wrapped around his hips, another in his hand.

"Here, this'll do the job," he said, kneeling by my side, placing the spare towel on my chest.

"Fine."

"I'm going to count to three, okay?" He wrapped his fingers around the handle.

"Okay." I clenched my jaw so tight my teeth hurt and closed my eyes.

"One—" He pulled the blade out and pressed the towel to the wound. I barely had time to register the pain before there was a thud, and Calder muttered, "What the hell?"

I opened my eyes to see Flynn, passed out by my side.

Fifteen

"Is he okay?"

"He… fainted," Calder said in disbelief. "I've never known a rat to have an aversion to blood."

"Given your feelings about rodents, I suspect you don't know many rats," I reminded him. "Also, you're a *bear*?" I was still getting my head around it. There was no other explanation for how Calder happened to be in my house, stark naked, when moments earlier a big black grizzly bear had been rampaging after Dino. They were one and the same. Sheriff Joshua Calder was a bear shifter. "Why didn't Doris tell me?" I whispered to myself.

Calder, who'd been pressing the towel against my wound, cautiously lifted the cloth to assess the injury. "How's it feeling?"

"Like I've just been stabbed. Don't suppose you're a healer too, by any chance?"

He shook his head, resumed the pressure with the

towel. I figured I was losing a fair amount of blood as I was starting to feel lightheaded, but then, my poor old skull had taken quite a pounding this evening. It wouldn't surprise me to learn I had a concussion.

"I'll call Doris," Calder said. Picking up one of my hands, he pressed it to the towel. "Hold this. Keep the pressure on." Releasing me, he scooped up Flynn and laid him on my stomach, then stood. "Where's your phone?"

"Around here somewhere. On the floor by the bed?" I turned my head to look, my vision blurring. I watched Calder's naked legs as he picked his way over the debris that had exploded over the living room, only there were two of him, swimming in and out of focus. As if coming from miles away and underwater, I heard Calder talking. Presumably to Doris.

Closing my eyes, I drifted in a warm cocoon, remembering the sight of Calder standing over me, practically stark naked, a familiar heat unfurling in my abdomen.

"Good grief! What happened here?" Doris had arrived, her bag hitting the floor by my head with a thump that echoed through my brain.

"Dino dropped in for a visit," I said, trying to pry my eyes open, but failing. Exhaustion pulled at me. "Did you bring Advil?"

"I've always got Advil," Doris assured me. "Hold tight, Holly, we'll have you fixed up in no time. Here's your clothes, Calder. Put some pants on, then help me get her onto the cot."

I dearly wanted to open my eyes and watch Calder dress, then cursed myself up one side and down the other for being a pervert. But still, the guy was *built*, and it turned out I wasn't resistant to his charms. Flynn stirred, stood up, and leaped off my belly.

"Flynn?" I called. "You okay?"

Squeak.

"He's fine," Calder assured me. "Probably embarrassed he fainted."

"That's nothing. You should see him get drunk and puke."

"You got your rat drunk?"

"Calder," Doris warned. She didn't say anything further, but I figured they exchanged glances that spoke volumes. If only I could pry my eyes open and see for myself. Instead, I lay on the floor and listened to the sounds of Calder dressing, then moving to stand by my head, Doris at my feet.

"Ready?" Calder asked.

"Let's do it," Doris replied. She grabbed my ankles, Calder slid his hands beneath my armpits, and they lifted.

"Holy heck, she weighs a *ton*," Doris complained. "My God, girl, what have you been eating? Bricks?"

I would have shot back a pithy reply, but my jaw was clenched tight as fire tore through my shoulder, up my neck, and down my spine simultaneously. "Ow," I managed to whimper.

"Sorry," Calder murmured. "It'll be over soon."

"Bet you say that to all the girls." Doris snorted, and

I couldn't help the weak laugh that escaped. But he was right. Seconds later, I was on the cot, only slightly less firm than the floor had been.

Doris began fussing with my shoulder, lifting the towel away, cutting the tank that I'd worn to bed. Darn it, I had a limited supply of clothes, and now I was down a tank.

"What can I do?" Calder's voice was laced with concern, coming from the foot of the cot.

"Hot water and a clean washcloth." Doris poked and prodded at my wound, making me hiss. "Stop being such a baby. It's just a scratch." I laughed. Trust Doris to compare a stab wound to a scratch.

"Yeah, that's what I figured. So, whack a plaster on it, and we'll be done, yeah?"

"Absolutely." Then she put something on the wound that was akin to a red-hot poker, and it went deep, all the way through the torn layers of flesh and muscle. Burning, sizzling, flaying my flesh from the bones type of pain.

"This might sting a tad," she said, patting my good shoulder while she poured what had to be alcohol over my open wound.

"Just a tad," I wheezed before sucking in another breath, trying to breathe through the agony.

Cracking open an eye, I watched Doris sitting on the edge of the cot, busy threading a needle. "You're lucky. Just soft tissue damage. Missed any bones and major arteries. Stitch you up and you'll be good as new."

"You're not a healer then." My disappointment was

genuine. I'd been hoping for a little magic to speed things along. Instead, I got Doris with a darning needle.

"If we call for one, the SIA is bound to find out. Are you prepared for that?"

I turned my head away and screwed my eyes tightly closed. "Nope. Just do it." Doris was right, though. If the SIA found out a healer had been summoned for me, Harding would be furious, maybe even pull me from Gravestone, and despite everything, I was starting to like it here. As far as safe houses went, I had freedom. I wasn't locked in a house, guarded, unable to leave. And with the town itself shielding magic from being tracked, it was the perfect hideout. Not to mention my friendship with the older woman and the attraction burning inside for the hot sheriff. No, despite all my complaining to the contrary, I wasn't ready to leave Gravestone just yet.

Doris worked quickly, stitching my torn skin back together. "You've done this before," I grunted through the pain.

"A time or two. My time with the SIA was different from yours. We had limited access to healers. We had to make do with what we had in the field."

Eventually, the fire receded, leaving a dull ache in its wake. Cracking open an eye, I looked at Doris sitting on the edge of the cot, putting away her supplies. "All done?" I croaked.

"Just like new." She grinned, her lime green curlers bobbing in her stark white hair.

"How do you sleep in them?"

"You get used to it."

Calder appeared, wearing jeans and a T-shirt, Flynn on his shoulder. I could only stare. Had his aversion to rodents been an act all along? Seeing my wide-eyed disbelief, he shrugged and threw me what could only be described as a sheepish grin. "We've come to an understanding."

"Right." I rolled my eyes. "From bear to rat."

"Did you do all this?" Doris asked, standing up, purse hooked over her elbow.

"Just the front door. Sorry about that," he apologized, which was sweet but unnecessary, considering the state of the rest of the house.

"Dino and me got into it." Sitting up, I swung my legs off the side of the cot, the room swimming. "Whoa!"

"Take it easy there, tiger." Doris clamped a hand on my good shoulder to stop me from toppling over. "I stitched you up, but you're not healed yet. You need to take it easy." She turned to Calder. "What now? She can't stay here—there's no doors. And barely a wall."

Doris was right. Calder had busted through the front door, Dino had kicked down the back door, and Dino and I had crashed through the wall dividing the living room from the kitchen. The lower floor of my house was trashed.

"Can she stay with you until we get this place secured?" he suggested.

"Of course! What fun, a girly sleepover!" She clapped her hands together in glee, and I shot Calder a look—had I just gone from the frying pan into the fire? I'd never been in Doris's house before, but I'd seen the outside, with its multiple colors and blinking Christmas lights all year round. How her neighbors coped, I didn't know.

Calder helped me to my feet, keeping an arm around my waist as we followed Doris out to the Impala. It was nice having someone strong to lean against, and it occurred to me that I'd never leaned on anyone before. Once more, a feeling of contentment settled over me, unsettling me. *Don't get used to this. Once the hit on me is neutralized, I'll be back at work and leaving Gravestone behind... and everyone in it. Don't get attached.* I suspected it was already too late.

"I'll stay here for the rest of the night," Calder said, one arm resting on top of the car as he leaned down to talk to me through the passenger window. "Make sure the place is secure. I'll give Casey a call first thing. Get him to secure the doors."

I looked up into his face, so close to mine. "Thank you. For coming."

"Figured something was up when I woke up to your rat sitting on my chest slapping me."

I chuckled at the visual. "Flynn. His name is Flynn."

"And he's not a rat." It wasn't a question.

"No. But then, you *are* a bear."

His eyes narrowed. "That isn't common knowledge, and I'd like to keep it that way."

"Understood." Who was I to blow his cover when my whole existence in this town was a lie?

"Take care." He surprised me by gently touching the back of his fingers against my cheek, and I closed my eyes, allowing myself, for the briefest of moments, to enjoy the pleasure of his touch, for I knew all too soon it would end.

Doris's house was… something else. It was bigger on the inside, for one. From the outside, it looked like a cottage, but from the sweeping staircase in the foyer to the grand rooms leading off it, it was more of a mansion. Enchanted for sure. And decorated in every garish Christmas decoration you could imagine and then some. Tinsel was woven around the balustrade on the staircase, along with holly and twinkling lights. There was a huge Christmas tree in the foyer that dominated the space, while a soft snowfall drifted down over the tree.

"You live in a snow globe." It was pretty, but it was a lot. Flynn jumped from my shoulder and headed off to explore.

"Welcome to Casa de Doris." Doris beamed, twirling in a circle.

"Thanks for doing this."

"What else were you going to do? Stay at Calder's?"

I somehow had a feeling that if I slept at Joshua Calder's house, there'd be very little sleeping going on. It was probably for the best that I was here, yet a little piece of me yearned for what might have been.

"The spare room is already made up. I'll get you something to sleep in."

"Thanks." I followed her upstairs to the guest room. It was a large room with rose wallpaper and green carpet. There was yet another Christmas tree in the corner, a star on top emitting a soft glow. The comforter on the bed was of a Christmas scene with a tree and puppies. The pillowcases depicted a dog wearing a Santa hat.

"Bathroom is through here. You should take a shower and get cleaned up. The dressing on your shoulder is waterproof, but try to keep the water off it just in case. I'll leave some clothes on the bed for you. Good night, Holly."

"Goodnight, Doris." I smiled behind a yawn. I was beat. It had been one heck of a night, and I was physically and emotionally exhausted, but she was right, I couldn't climb between her crisp, clean sheets covered not only sweat and blood, but dust and filth from crashing through the wall. The bathroom, thankfully, was relatively normal, if not for the row of Santa's elves perched atop the mirrored cabinet. Ignoring them, I examined my reflection in the mirror. Battered and bruised, but still standing.

I examined my shoulder; the dressing covering the wound. Maybe I'd have a scar? I'd had plenty of injuries as an SIA agent, yet no scars marred my skin. Probably thanks to the healers the SIA used. I'd never really thought about it before. Funny how you don't miss something until it's gone.

Stripping out of my torn clothes, I stepped into the shower and stood with my back to the spray, allowing the water to flow over me as I relived the evening's events. I'd have to tell Doris about the Whelans' visit and that they were refugees from Purgatory, not looking for trouble but a quiet life to raise a family. Then there was Dino's visit. Maybe I shouldn't have confronted him? Maybe I should have let him think I was sleeping and allowed him to search the place, find the puzzle box. But it wasn't in my nature to do nothing. I'd had to take action, but had I inadvertently blown my cover? Would Dino know I was more than I said I was? And he kept calling me a little witch. Did he know, for sure, that I was a witch, or was it merely an insult?

Tired of all the questions for which I had no answers, I finished up in the shower and wrapped myself in a large fluffy towel. Padding into the bedroom, I stopped when I saw what was waiting for me on the bed. A Christmas onesie. Folded neatly next to it was a pair of leopard skin pants and a red T-shirt with *ho-ho-ho* printed on the front in gold glitter.

Pulling on the onesie, I wrapped my hair in the towel and climbed into bed. I was asleep almost as soon as my head hit the pillow.

CHAPTER
Sixteen

"Rise and shine!" Doris yanked open the curtains in the guest bedroom, bright sunlight hitting me directly in the face.

Raising my arm to shield my eyes, I struggled to calm my racing heart from the abrupt awakening. I'd been sound asleep mere seconds ago. "What time is it?"

"Six. Coffee?"

Cautiously peering through one eye, I eyeballed the crazy woman who I'd become ridiculously fond of. The lime green curlers were gone, her white hair styled in elegant waves, red lipstick in place. She wore a psychedelic-colored body suit with a pair of bright blue slacks and orthopedic sandals.

"Who are you dressed as?"

She grinned and practically bounded across the room. At the door, she turned. "Coffee is ready downstairs. Hurry up, we've got some catching up to do."

Throwing back the covers, I eased myself out of bed. My body ached like I'd done ten rounds with Mike Tyson. Trying not to groan with every step, I hobbled across the room to the bathroom before getting dressed in the clothes Doris had left the night before. Sans underwear, because there was no way I was wearing Doris's panties.

"Are your knees supposed to sound like a goat chewing on an aluminum can stuffed with celery?" I asked, easing myself onto a chair at Doris's dining room table.

"You're just stiff. You'll loosen up in no time." Doris placed a cup of coffee in front of me, and I gratefully wrapped my hands around it.

"Your house is so cool." I'd noticed it last night, the lack of heat. She either had amazing insulation and super silent air-conditioning, or like I'd suspected the night before, the house was enchanted.

"Thank you!" She preened, and I realized she'd thought I was complimenting her décor, not the temperature. The Christmas theme continued in the dining room, with elves as salt and pepper shakers, a bowl full of pinecones painted red and green and liberally dipped in glitter, and paper daisy chains dangling from the curtain rails.

But enough of the decor. It was time to get down to business. "Why did you lie to me about Calder being human?"

Her impossibly long eyelashes swept down, hiding

her eyes, before she looked up, locking her gaze on me. "I thought he was."

"I can't tell if you're lying," I admitted, watching her shrug and take a sip of her coffee, leaving red lipstick on the rim of the cup.

"There has never been a bear sighting in Gravestone. As far as I was aware—and I'd never heard anything to the contrary—Calder was a bona fide human being."

"Now we know different."

She inclined her head. "Now we know different. How do you feel?"

My head snapped up, and I shot her a glare. "What do you mean, how do I feel? I don't care! He can be anything he likes." Truth was, I didn't know how I felt. I just knew that Calder was creeping under my defenses, and I kinda liked it. That had me twitchy and uncomfortable but was also warming in a soft-centered chocolate kind of way.

"I meant how do you feel, as in, how's your shoulder? And foot?"

"Oh!" My hand automatically shot to the stab wound. "Fine. It's not too bad. But then, everything aches right now." The bruises on my face weren't as bad as they'd been the night before. I'd been worried I'd be sporting two black eyes today. As it was, I just looked like I'd been dabbling in Goth makeup.

My foot ached but then it always ached. "We need to get my walking boot," I said, remembering I'd left it by the side of my bed when Dino had turned up. Which reminded me, I hadn't told Doris about my earlier visitors.

"The Whelans came to visit me last night."

"They did?"

"Yeah. The ward in the upstairs bedroom was broken. From when we were in there packing up the books—I had the window open, and when we closed it, it must have blown the salt away."

"I told you to check your wards." Doris tossed her head, as if flipping her hair, if her hair were long enough to flip, that is.

"Yes, you did. And I did downstairs. But silly me, didn't think anyone would gain entry upstairs."

"So, they came in through the bedroom window. What happened?"

I filled her in on what the Whelans told me, about escaping from Purgatory and their desire for a peaceful life in Gravestone.

"Of course, they're not going to do anything to jeopardize that. So, they didn't kill Cody." She finished her coffee, placing the cup back on the table with a thump.

"Nope." I fiddled with the salt and pepper shakers, moving them back and forth. "And I don't think Dino did either. Not only did I overhear him telling Kerris he didn't do it, but he admitted he was with the mayor at the time of the murder."

"What was he doing with the mayor?"

"Things you don't want to know."

Her eyes grew wide. "You mean they were—"

I cut her off, nodding. "Yep. So the Whelans didn't do it. Dino didn't do it."

Doris reached forward and grabbed the pepper shaker, moving it to the right. "That leaves Keelan Moore. He must have killed Cody."

"We just need to prove it." I eyeballed the pepper shaker. "What's his motive?"

"Well, Cody did sell the puzzle box that Keelan had paid him to get."

"Cody didn't sell it. Macey did. By accident," I reminded her. "So, it wouldn't make sense for Keelan to kill Cody. Instead, he'd put pressure on Cody to get the box back. Killing him would mean he wouldn't get what he wanted."

Doris snorted. "Keelan could easily hire someone else to retrieve the box. He knew where it was. He knew you bought it from Macey at the market. He didn't *need* Cody. Maybe he roughed him up, wanting his money back, and things got out of hand?"

"Keelan doesn't strike me as the type to let things get out of hand." No. Keelan Moore was a smooth operator. I remembered the charm he was using at River's café. Everyone was under his spell. Except me. "But I agree. I think Keelan charmed someone into breaking into my house to steal the box."

"You think he's your intruder?"

"Not Keelan directly. But he's using magic for sure. You don't remember, do you?"

"Remember what?"

"At River's café? When he approached our table?"

"He did?"

"Keelan Moore has some sort of magical ability to bend people to his will without them knowing or remembering."

"Oooooh, you're saying he spelled someone to break into your house to get the box?"

"Yes! Exactly." I nodded. "And then he had Cody killed to send a message. You don't mess with Keelan Moore and live to talk about it."

Doris surged to her feet. "Let's go tell Calder."

I remained seated, shaking my head. "Only one problem. We have no evidence. And that's the first thing Calder is going to say. *Where's your proof?*"

"Proof smoof." Doris waved away my concerns. "Keelan is staying at Joan Jackson's B&B. Let's go find the proof we need."

Flynn jumped onto the table, sitting in front of me. Today, he was green and red, matching the theme of Doris's house. "Hey, Flynn, how are you?" I hadn't really had a chance to talk to him since the attack. "Thanks for getting Calder last night. Things got kinda hairy."

Flynn nodded and pointed to my shoulder. "My shoulder? It's fine. Like Doris said, he didn't do any major damage. But you… you fainted. What was that all about?"

Flynn stood on his hind legs, planted his front paws

on his hips, and squeaked up a tirade, of which I understood nothing. Eventually, he ran out of steam, gave a decisive nod, and fled.

"What did he say?" Doris asked.

Standing up, I looked toward the door Flynn had disappeared through. "I have no idea, but I think he was denying he fainted. Come on then, let's go see if Keelan is home."

"We can stop at River's for breakfast after." Picking up her oversized bag, Doris hustled to the front door, whereas I followed along at a slower pace, every muscle hurting. Maybe I'd take a salt bath later, ease some of the soreness. Wasn't as if I didn't have plenty of salt on hand.

"I'm a little fuzzy," I confessed from the passenger seat of the Impala. "Did Calder say he'd call Casey for me? To secure the house?"

"Affirmative." Resting her hand on the back of my seat, she looked over her shoulder as she reversed out of the driveway at breakneck speed. I couldn't contain the whimper as the sudden braking and changing of gears flung me back against the seat, my hand instinctively going to my shoulder.

"Oops. Sorry. Forgot."

"Where is Joan's B&B?" Hopefully not too far away. I wasn't sure I was up to one of Doris's drives today.

"Just up here." Doris pointed out the windshield. "She lives in the house in front and rents out the apartment out back." Literally thirty seconds later, we rolled past Joan's house. It was beautiful. And right on the foreshore, with no street access to the front of the property.

I examined the house and the apartment as we slowly drove past. The apartment opened directly onto the street, giving the occupant their own private access without disturbing Joan.

"Does Keelan have a car?" I asked Doris, not seeing any vehicles parked in front of the B&B.

"I'd imagine he would have. Gravestone isn't known for its public transport." Doris executed a seven-point turn and drove back, pulling to a stop on the opposite side of the road. "Ready?"

I held out my hand, palm up. Doris looked at it. "What?"

I raised a brow. "Lock pick?"

"Right, right." Rummaging in her bag, she produced a leather pouch and slapped it into my palm. "There you go."

"I'll be right back. Keep a lookout." I slid out of the car with an audible groan, then crossed the road, looking this way and that, keeping my eyes peeled for any signs of life. Or Keelan. It was early, most people were still in their homes, but I couldn't discount some zealous jogger would find this the perfect time of day to get their morning exercise in.

One more furtive glance over my shoulder, and with the coast clear, I picked the lock. Slipping inside, I quietly closed the door behind me. The front door opened directly into a small open plan living room and kitchenette. A quick glance told me Keelan was either an incredibly clean and tidy person or he'd already left because there was nothing here to indicate anyone was currently in residence. The cushions were strategically placed on the sofa, no indentations to show someone had leaned against them recently. The kitchen was immaculate; the sink showing not even a water stain.

A search of the cupboards and drawers revealed nothing. I headed for the bedroom. The queen-size bed didn't look like it had been slept in, and I was starting to think I was right that Keelan had already checked out when I opened the wardrobe and found clothes hanging there. Men's clothes.

"Bingo." I was patting down the shirts and trousers, hoping to find something, anything, when I heard the front door open. *Crap!* Where was Doris? She was supposed to be keeping a lookout! Then I heard it. A belated cock-a-doodle-doo. *Really, Doris? A rooster?*

I briefly considered hiding in the wardrobe, but it was too small, one narrow closet with two drawers beneath it. Which left the bed. Dropping to the floor, I rolled under, wincing at the protest in my shoulder, holding my breath when a pair of men's shoes came into view. Pressing my hand over my mouth to keep silent, I watched as they walked past the end of the bed to the wardrobe, bit my lip when I heard the wardrobe door close. In my haste to hide, I'd left it open. I was hoping Keelan would think he'd left it open, but no such luck.

"You may as well come out. I know you're under the bed."

My forehead hit the floor. From outside, I heard another cock-a-doodle-doo. Nice try, Doris, but a little late. It was my own fault for not coming up with another method for her to warn me. As it was, I didn't have my phone—in fact, I didn't know where it was and just assumed it was still at my house. Last night was a bit of a blur.

"You can come out under your own steam," Keelan drawled, "or I can drag you out."

"Okay, okay," I grumbled, rolling out from under the bed, ignoring the pull of my stitches. I lay on the carpet and looked up at Keelan standing over me. I was surprised he was surprised.

"Holly Day, I did not expect it to be you."

"Oh? Why not?" I clambered to my feet but had nowhere to go. Trapped between the bed and the wall, Keelan blocking the exit. "Were you expecting someone else?"

"In my line of work, I'm always expecting someone else." Apparently, he didn't see me as a threat, for he turned his back and walked away. "To what do I owe the pleasure?" he called as he made his way to the kitchen.

Deciding I had nothing to lose by laying my cards on the table, I opted for the truth. "Searching for evidence that you killed Cody Pendant."

He was fiddling with the coffee maker when I joined

him. Glancing at me over his shoulder, he asked, "Find any?"

I shook my head. "Sadly, no."

He laughed. "That's because I didn't kill him. Why would I?"

"Oh, I don't know, maybe because he sold the puzzle box to me when you'd commissioned him to get it for you."

"Ahh." He pointed a teaspoon at me. "But he didn't. Sell it, that is. It was Macey who sold it to you. So, if that's your reasoning, maybe I should kill her? Or you."

He had me there, and truth be told, I hadn't been able to think of a plausible motive for Keelan killing Cody other than they were both crooks, and why not? While I stood there pondering the ins and outs of the underworld both men moved in, I felt the change in the air. Thick. Warm. Tingly. He was using magic.

While he waited for his coffee to brew, he turned and leaned back against the sink, arms crossed over his chest, watching me. "Speaking of the puzzle box," he drawled, voice deep, low, seductive. "Where is it?"

"I've already told you your magic doesn't work on me, so you're wasting your time. Do you have an alibi for when Cody was killed?"

"I was here."

"Alone?"

His lips curled up in a sly smile. "Perhaps."

"Look, if you had a *lady friend* with you, then you should tell me. If she can confirm she was with you, then you'd have an alibi, and I'd take you off my list of suspects."

His eyes narrowed. "Who are you? SIA?"

Crap. "More like an amateur sleuth," I blurted. "I was dragged into this whole mess against my will, and someone needs to sort it out."

The coffee machine beeped, and he turned toward it. "It may as well be you, eh?"

"It may as well be me," I agreed. I wasn't paying attention to what Keelan was doing, and I should have been. Between one breath and the next, he was across the room with a knife to my throat. I let out a startled squeak while the rooster continued to crow outside.

"My magic may not work on you," he growled, breath hot on my face, "but this knife can cut you. What do you have to say about that?"

I looked him dead in the eye and for the life of me, I don't know why I said it, but I did. "Ever thought of a breath mint?"

He laughed, caressed my neck with the blade, running it softly across my skin. "You're funny, I'll give you that. And either brave or stupid, I haven't decided which." Lowering the knife, he stepped away. "Coffee?"

To hide the fact that my knees were trembling and about to give way, I took a seat at the table. "Sure, why not?" For the life of me, I couldn't work Keelan out. One minute he blew hot, the next cold.

Carrying two cups to the table, Keelan sat opposite me. "I have a proposition for you. A deal."

"Oh?" I eyed the coffee cup he'd placed in front of

me, wondering if it was poisoned. As if reading my mind, he picked it up, took a sip, then set it back down in front of me before taking a mouthful from his own cup. "Satisfied?"

I nodded, a little embarrassed that he'd read me so easily. He was running rings around me, and it was irritating. "What sort of deal?"

"Information in exchange for the puzzle box."

"What sort of information? I get the feeling you're trying to trick me."

"I was with Macey the night her father died," he said, leaning back in his chair, watching me with dark eyes.

"You're sleeping with Macey Pendant?" I was shocked. He was twice her age.

"Not sleeping. Doing business with. You see, Cody was grooming Macey to take over the business. He had plans to retire. Macey is a smarter girl than her father ever gave her credit for. She's selling the business. To me. My boss thinks it would be a good acquisition."

Yeah, for fencing stolen antiquities, I was sure. "Is that why you were at the café with her? Finalizing the deal after her father's rather timely murder?"

Keelan inclined his head, "In a manner of speaking."

Cock-a-doodle-dooooooo.

"Do you want to invite your friend in?" Keelan asked.

I downed my coffee in one go, burning my esophagus. My eyes teared up, and I blinked, struggling to my feet. Holy heck, but it hurt to even breathe through the fire ravaging my throat. "Thanks for the intel," I rasped. "Most helpful."

Keelan was on his feet too, and, hand wrapped around my throat, propelled me into the door. He moved fast. Way faster than a witch, wizard, or warlock moved. Through the pressure on my throat that was firm but not painful, I swallowed, for a thought had popped into my head, and now that it was there, I couldn't dislodge it. *Vampire.*

"Oh, no. You don't get information for free." His breath was hot on my face, and again, I felt the urge to suggest a breath mint, but I was getting the feeling Keelan Moore was getting tired of playing Mr. Nice Guy. His patience was running out. Which was precisely what he said next.

"My patience is running out. Where is the puzzle box?"

If Keelan was a vampire, he was a powerful one, a day walker. It would explain the hypnotic effect he had on people. It would explain his speed. I didn't realize I was staring intently at his mouth, searching for a glimpse of fangs, until he lifted me off the ground by my throat just to get my attention. I clawed at his hand, legs dangling, struggling to breathe.

"The box! Now!" His eyes glowed red, and when his lips curled back in a snarl, I saw what I'd been looking for. Yep. Vampire, all right. Usually, when I dealt with vampires, I had a pyre gun and protective gear. To say I was at a disadvantage was an understatement. But I was running out of options, as well as oxygen, as I dangled from his grip like a rag doll. With black spots starting to appear, I brought my legs up and kicked. Hard. He hadn't been expecting the move and while he didn't release his hold, he did lose his balance, and we crashed to the floor, where my head slammed against the tiles and I saw stars. Was it bad to get a concussion on top of a concussion? Probably.

Keelan was upon me in a millisecond, sitting on my chest, knees pinning my arms to the floor. I was beat. He knew it. I knew it. Doris, the rooster impersonator outside, did not know it and was continuing to crow up a storm. I wished she'd quit it and realize I was actually in trouble and go get help. Heaven forbid she'd try to help me herself. I'd already seen the effect Keelan had on her. She'd be no use to me whatsoever. Instead, she'd do his bidding. I wasn't sure if it would be ironic or horrifying if he instructed her to kill me—all so he didn't have to get his hands dirty, of course. But then, if I was dead, he'd never get his hands on the puzzle box. I had one bargaining chip left.

"Okay," I wheezed. "I'll get the puzzle box."

"Your word is your bond?" He lowered his face to mine until our noses were practically touching. It was most disconcerting. I went cross-eyed trying to meet his eyes.

"Yes." I was doing a deal with a gangster. A thug. But Keelan didn't know what I knew—and didn't think to even ask—had I opened the box? The answer, of course, was a resounding yes. So, technically, he could have the box. But the soul stone that had been hidden inside stayed with me.

He leaped off me, leaving me breathless—not in a good way—on the floor. Rolling to my side, I used the wall to pull myself to my feet, straightening my Christmas tee and dusting off the leopard print pants. My shoulder throbbed.

"You have one hour to deliver the box."

"Fine." Opening the door, I stepped outside, halting Doris's cock-a-doodle-doo mid squawk.

CHAPTER
Seventeen

"Well?" Doris demanded, keeping step with me as I hurried as fast as my battered and bruised body would allow back to her car. "What happened?" She'd been hiding, not very successfully, behind a tree.

"Later," I hissed, knowing Keelan would be listening. Which meant I had to distract Doris before she blurted out something we didn't want him to know. "Can we swing by my place before we go to River's? My foot is killing me. I really need my walking boot." It wasn't a lie. My foot ached, but I could have managed without the boot for a little longer.

"Oh, yes, of course." Doris slung her arm around my waist. "Here, lean on me."

I did, letting her help me to the Impala. As soon as we were clear of Keelan and I was confident he couldn't hear us, I said, "He's a vampire."

Doris slammed her foot on the brakes, squealing to a stop in the middle of the road. "What?"

I nodded, hand gripping the dash. "Uh-huh. He's a vampire. That's what he was using in the café, not magic per se, but glamor."

"But… he was out walking around in the sun."

"Day walker," I explained. "But he mentioned having a boss, so I'm thinking he's not all that powerful. He's probably wearing some sort of charm that allows him to move about during the day."

"Well, isn't that just pooptastic? That changes things." She moved her foot from the brake and back onto the accelerator, jolting me backward in my seat.

"Not really." Clutching the door handle, I held on when she swung onto Berryman Street. "He *didn't* kill Cody. No vampire would waste that much blood, nor leave a body behind. I think he would have put pressure on Cody to get the puzzle box back from me. It would be a pride thing. No Arzan would let him off the hook like that."

"So Keelan didn't kill Cody?"

"I don't believe so, no. And I don't think he ordered someone else to do it. He wanted Cody alive to get the soul stone. After that? Who knows? Maybe Cody would have disappeared." I suspected that either way, Cody was destined to reach a sticky end, but if Keelan had been behind his death, I doubted very much he'd still be in town. No. He still had business to take care of, and that business was me.

We pulled to a stop in front of my house, parking behind Casey's truck.

"Doris, I need you to stay away from Keelan Moore. Because he can compel you to tell him the truth. Right now, he doesn't know we got the puzzle box open, and I want him to keep on thinking that. I've agreed to give him the box. I'm hoping he won't know how to solve the puzzle either and he'll be a long way from Gravestone when he finally gets it open—or someone opens it for him—and that he'll think that Cody tricked him or whoever Cody got the puzzle box from did. I want you and me well and truly out of the equation."

She looked hurt. "You think I'd give us away?"

"I don't think you'd mean to…"

"Okay, fine." She pouted. "So, what's the plan?"

"I get my walking boot and the box, and we go have breakfast at River's."

"And you're going to hand over the box. Just like that?"

If only it were that simple. I'd had no doubt Keelan was prepared to kill me and tear apart my house to get the box, and I kinda liked being alive. "You and I both know the box itself isn't what's important," I reminded her. "But yes, I'm handing over the box. I put on a good show of not wanting to give it to him, but in the end, he persuaded me that it was the best course of action." *If I wanted to keep on breathing.*

"Where is the handover taking place?"

"He would have heard me tell you our plan. Come get the walking boot, breakfast at River's. I'm pretty sure he'll turn up while we're there. He's a smart man. He'd have noticed I didn't mention the puzzle box to you, that I intend to pick it up at the same time as my boot, so he's going to think you're not involved." I crossed my fingers that I could keep Doris out of the handover. Of course, he knew she was crowing like a rooster outside of his accommodation. I just hoped he thought that was the extent of her involvement. In this situation, Doris was the weak link, not that I could ever tell her that. I'd never hear the end of it.

"Mornin' Holly, mornin' Doris." Casey stepped out of my house. "How are you two ladies doing this morning? Calder told me there was some excitement here last night." He waved the hammer in his hand, indicating the broken door behind him.

"Yeah, you could say that." Climbing out of the car, I approached. "Sorry to call you out like this."

"You okay?" His eyes looked extra blue today, coupled with his dirty blond hair, square jaw, and tanned skin. He was, quite frankly, delicious. Seeing him didn't have my heart skipping a beat the same way it did whenever I laid eyes on Calder, but that didn't mean I didn't enjoy the eye candy.

"I'm fine. Just dropped by to pick up a few things." I turned to Doris, following behind. "Is it okay if I do some laundry at your house?"

"Of course."

Casey stepped aside to let us pass. "I'll get new doors installed, and I'll clear up the demolished wall, but I can't officially begin the renovations until we get that permit from the council."

"No problem. Kerris assured me it'd be in your mailbox in a day or two."

I was taken aback at the destruction inside. I'd known we'd made a mess of things, but seeing the damage in the cold light of day was sobering. Three quarters of the kitchen wall was missing, torn apart when Dino plowed me through it. There was a dry blood stain on the living room floor where the knife he'd meant for Calder had missed its target and hit me instead.

Doris ran her hand up and down my back. "Chin up, it coulda been worse."

"Really? How?" I gave her a weak smile.

"Coulda been a dragon." She winked. "How about you get what you need down here, and I'll get whatever you need from upstairs?"

"Just my dirty laundry from the back bedroom. Toss it all in the suitcase."

"No problemo." She shot up the stairs with a spring in her step while I sat on the cot and strapped on my walking boot. I glanced up to find Casey watching me.

"I found something," he said. Leaning over, he picked up a leather-bound notebook from the camp chair and handed it to me. Turning it over in my hands, I could see that it was old, weathered, much used.

"I found it in the wall cavity," Casey continued. "Figured you might be interested."

I looked up at him. "Do you think it was John's? That he hid it?"

He shrugged. "Maybe? Because the wall is all busted up, I couldn't really identify if he had some sort of secret panel or opening to allow access. It may have been accidentally left in there when the place was being built."

The look on his face told me he didn't believe it any more than I did. Who accidentally left a book in a wall?

"Did you read it?" I unwrapped the leather cord and opened the book. It was filled with handwritten notes, names, sketches, and drawings. Whoever the notebook belonged to, they had exceptional penmanship. A particular sketch caught my eye, and I paused for a minute to admire it. It was of a woman, cradling a seal, her long hair flowing around them.

"This is the same as the statue in the town square," I said.

"The sea wolf statue?" Casey asked, peering at the book upside down.

"Sea wolf?"

"Yeah, the statue was erected in honor of Marilla, a mermaid who lived in the mangroves," Casey told me. "The seal is her offspring, Earendil. They co-habited happily with humans until Christopher Columbus discovered a taste for them—he referred to seals as sea wolves and killed them for their meat."

I blanched. How… gross.

"When Earendil was slaughtered, Marilla and her fellow mermaids created havoc by luring fishermen to their deaths, causing great storms, and generally bestowing bad luck on anyone who should see one."

"But the statue in town… the woman, Marilla, is wearing a dress." I'd never guessed for a second that she was a mermaid. "Why not show her tail?"

"Superstition. Even a statue depicting an actual mermaid is enough to bring bad luck."

"Why erect a statue at all if it's risky?"

"It's more of a memorial for Earendil to appease her."

"Guessing by the number of storms that roll through Gravestone, I don't think it's working."

Casey chuckled. "Fair point."

Closing the book, I wrapped the leather cord around it and slid it into my backpack, thinking I'd check it out later at Doris's place. Casey remained where he was, standing over me, and I looked back at him, brows raised.

"You don't want trouble with the Tarkaths," he said solemnly.

"You know about the Tarkaths?" That was a surprise.

He nodded once. "Calder told me Dino Cittadino is behind this. Dino runs with the Tarkaths. Therefore he is bad news. You don't want to mess with them."

I sighed. "I know." Which was another reason why I was prepared to give Keelan what he wanted. With the puzzle box gone, I'd no longer be a target. Neither the Tarkaths or the Arzans needed to know I had the soul stone, and as long as Doris could keep her mouth shut, we'd be fine. I pondered reaching out to Harding, asking the SIA to come to take possession of the stone. That would take care of all my problems. Well, all my current problems. There was still a hit out on me and until that threat was neutralized, I was still required to hide out in Gravestone. But if I was to maintain my cover, I needed the Tarkaths and Arzans gone before they stumbled upon the truth.

"It's fine," I assured him. "It's sorted." I held his gaze, unblinking, until he gave a slight nod and resumed his journey out to his truck.

There was no sign of my phone, but I grabbed the charger and laptop. I shoved them into my backpack with the old notebook, then rummaged in the freezer for the puzzle box, shoving that in too. I planned on spending the day at Doris's house, getting my laundry done, and being back in my own house by nightfall. Keelan would have the puzzle box and word would reach those who needed to hear it that it was no longer in my possession. All that was left to do was find Cody's killer, and as much as I'd like to tie it all up in a pretty little bow, I did not think either the Tarkaths nor the Arzans were responsible.

But the information Keelan had given me was more useful than he realized. Macey Pendant was about to take over the family business and then sell it behind her father's back. What if Cody caught wind of those plans? What if he decided not to hand over the reins to Macey? She'd be furious. And also screwed, financially. But was she capable of killing her father? I wasn't so sure. I'd seen the way Cody treated her, but I'd also seen that she was a woman who'd been conditioned by this man her entire life. She knew no other way than to obey him, to do as she was told.

The thump, thump, thump of my suitcase on the staircase heralded Doris's descent. Meeting her at the foot of the stairs, I led the way outside. Casey was at the back of his truck and looked up, watching as we approached, his eyes sparkling in the bright morning sun. If only it was him who had my heart doing somersaults. It would have been easy. A no strings dalliance while I was in Gravestone, a bit of fun, then I'd be on my way. But no, my traitorous body yearned for someone other than Casey. Someone complicated. Someone with secrets. Someone who, I just knew, was already worming their way into my heart and would make leaving that much harder.

"Here." Casey smiled, holding out two keys dangling from a ring. "Better take these so you can get in when you come back."

"Thanks, Casey. Appreciate it." Accepting the keys, I went to tuck them in my pocket before remembering I was wearing Doris's leopard print pants that had no pockets.

Casey watched me pat myself down. "Nice pants," he drawled. "Quite the look for you."

I laugh snorted. "Thanks. They're Doris's, as if you didn't know." Pretty sure the whole town knew Doris's penchant for leopard print. Securing the keys in the front pocket of my backpack, I tossed it on the back seat of the Impala. "I'll spend the day at Doris's, take advantage of her washing machine while I can."

Leaning one elbow on the side of his truck, Casey crossed his feet at the ankles and cocked his head. "I can order you a washing machine if you like? And install it as part of the renovation. John used to have one in the mud room, but it rusted out."

"Sure, that'd be great."

"Let me know what make and model you want." Straightening up, he returned his attention to whatever he was fiddling with in the tray of his truck.

"I don't really care. You choose. Something simple. Not too many dials or buttons."

"Roger." He didn't look up, just gave an absent wave.

I climbed into the passenger seat while Doris heaved my suitcase into the trunk and then we were on our way to River's. Ignoring the knots in my stomach as we approached at breakneck speed, I said to Doris, "When Keelan turns up, I need you to make yourself scarce. Make an excuse and go to the ladies' room or remember something you have to get from the car."

"Why?"

"Because he can influence you, and I don't want you accidentally telling him we got the box open."

"Oh, yeah. That. Okie dokie."

Parking in front of River's, we headed inside. It was early. Very early. We were the only customers, which, for some reason made me even more nervous. "Why am

I nervous?" I whispered to myself. Doris must've heard me, for she shot me a look but didn't say anything.

"Wow, look at you two early birds," River greeted us, looking me up and down. "That's a new look for you, Holly."

I glanced down at myself, grinning ruefully. "I'm officially out of clean clothes. Had to borrow some of Doris's until I get my laundry done."

"And Flynn?" She glanced out the window at Doris's Impala.

"He's at my house," Doris piped up. "Given how much laundry this one has to do, we figured we'd better fortify ourselves with a big breakfast first."

River laughed. "I hear ya on that, Holly. I'm always so busy with this place that doing laundry is way down on my list. Do y'all know what you want, or should I give you a minute?"

I glanced at Doris. "The usual?"

She nodded. "The usual."

"Eggs and pancakes with two pieces of bacon and a caramel latte for you, Doris." River didn't even write it down. "Hmmm, Holly, you always choose something different, so I'm not sure what your usual is."

"I'll have the same as her."

I was too wired to worry about what to eat. As it was, I wasn't sure I could eat anything my stomach was churning that badly. We were at our usual table, my backpack sitting on the chair next to me, when the bell over the door jangled. I knew without looking that

Keelan Moore had just walked in. The change in the air was immediate and powerful.

"Doris," I hissed. "Go powder your nose."

"Huh?" She looked at me like I had two heads, then turned and saw Keelan. "Oh. Right." Making a big show of standing up and grabbing her purse, she announced over-loudly, "I'm just going to refresh my lipstick."

"Okay." I watched her scuttle away to the bathroom, saw the smirk on Keelan's face as he approached and slid into the chair Doris had just vacated.

"Do you have it?" he asked without preamble.

Nodding, I reached for my backpack and pulled out the puzzle box, placing it on the table between us. Keelan picked it up, studying it intently. I was glad I'd thought to put a rock inside, to replace the soul stone. Until the box was opened, no one would know any different.

With a decisive nod, Keelan tossed a fifty-dollar bill on the table, stood with the box tucked under his arm, and said, "That's to cover your costs. Wouldn't want to be seen as owing you." Before I could answer, he strode out, the bell jangling once more. River, who'd been on her way to our table with an order pad in hand, stopped. "Oh. I thought he was joining you for breakfast."

I shook my head. "Nah. I decided to sell him the puzzle box that Macey accidentally sold me. Everyone had their panties in a twist over it. I figured I'd let her off the hook."

"The poor girl was really upset about that," River confided. "Apparently, her dad was really mad at her about it. She was saying her last words with him were them fighting."

"Do you know them well? Cody and Macey?"

River shrugged. "A little. They were always as thick as thieves, those two. I got the feeling they had a lot of scams going on. Macey is quite the actress, often playing the victim to fleece their marks out of more money. I think Cody would set them up, then Macey would do her thing."

She spun on her heel and returned to the kitchen while I pondered what she'd just told me, specifically, that Macey was quite the actress. Was the scene that I'd witnessed at the market an act? Meant to illicit sympathy? But to what end? If I'd given them the puzzle box, I'd have demanded a full refund, so what was in it for them?

I was still pondering it when Doris returned, her lips an interesting shade of purple. "What happened to you?" I asked.

"Has he gone? Is it done?" she whispered, looking around furtively as she took her seat.

I nodded. "Yes, it's all done and yes, he's gone. You can relax." But just in case he was loitering within earshot, I raised a finger to my lips in warning not to discuss the soul stone. "Tell me about your lipstick," I invited, as a way of distraction. "I don't think I've seen that shade on you before."

"No, well." She cleared her throat and squared her

shoulders. "It's three shades. And they kinda blended into… this. I kinda like it. What do you think?"

"I think it's… different. And you. Definitely you. Although your usual red matches the theme of your house more than the purple does."

"Yes! That's exactly what I thought," she declared, before launching into a TED Talk about lipstick shades. I let my mind drift as she talked until we were interrupted by River with our breakfast.

"Before you go…" I reached out and touched her wrist after she'd placed my plate of pancakes and bacon in front of me. A zap of electricity shot up my arm from where we touched, and I snatched my hand back in shock.

"Sorry." River rubbed her wrist. "Static electricity. I'm always zapping people. Was there something you wanted?"

"What you said before about Macey? I know they travel down to the market every month, but do they stay over?"

"Sure, sometimes. They've got a storage facility on Thuruna Road that they use occasionally, and I think Macey has been staying at the RV park and campground because Calder told her she couldn't leave town yet."

I smiled tightly. "Thanks, River. This looks—and smells—delicious." Now that my meeting with Keelan had passed without incident, my appetite had returned with a vengeance, and I dug in, the pancakes melting in my mouth, the bacon just the right amount of crispy.

As if reading my mind, Doris waved her fork at me and said with her mouth full, "What happens now? With Keelan?"

"Nothing happens. The saga with the puzzle box is done. We never managed to get it open. He gave me what I paid for it. Good luck to him."

"But we—"

"Didn't get it open," I repeated, shooting her a glare. I really hoped she wasn't getting dementia. The last thing I needed was her running around blabbing about the soul stone to all and sundry.

"No, I know we didn't," she snapped, eyes flashing. "I was going to say we should have held out for more money. I'm sure he would've coughed up a hundred."

I was silent for a second before bursting out laughing. "Yeah, well, to be honest, I'm glad to be rid of it. It was more trouble than it was worth. Hopefully, people will stop breaking into my house now."

Eighteen

"I can see the cogs turning from here," Doris said, waving her fork at me again. "You think we should pay Macey a visit."

"As tempting as that is, I think we need to regroup first. Dino is around the place somewhere, and I'd prefer not to get jumped by him again anytime soon. Let's go back to your house, do my laundry, and work out a plan of action. Plus, I need Advil." It wasn't a lie. Now that the adrenaline rush had receded, my head was pounding. Add to that my collection of aches and pains, and I felt like I could sleep for a week.

"You do look peaky. One of my herbal teas should perk you right up."

We left the café and returned to Doris's house. It felt good to be rid of the puzzle box, like a weight had been lifted, and I was relieved I hadn't had to bring it with me to Doris's house. She didn't need that sort of trouble. The knowledge that the soul stone was safely hidden in the tree behind my house was comforting, too.

Cradling the herbal concoction Doris had made in my palms, I was two sips in and already feeling better. Of course, it tasted like dirt, and I had to hold my nose to keep from gagging, but I trusted her not to poison me.

"Better?" she asked. We were sitting in the living room, in two armchairs facing the window with a wonderful view of the ocean. Christmas mayhem surrounded us, with oversized boxes and massive candy canes as decorations.

"Much. Thank you."

I could tell she was bursting to tell me something. Either that or all the fidgeting meant she needed to go to the bathroom. "Yes?" I asked, caving.

"Hmmm?" Her head bobbled, and she crossed and uncrossed her legs.

"Do you need to wee?"

"What? No!"

"Then spit it out. Whatever you want to say, because all that wriggling about looks like you're about to wet your pants," I teased, feeling more and more relaxed by the minute.

She leaned forward, elbows on knees, eyes intent. "I mean, it has to be Macey, right? She's the only suspect we have left who could have killed Cody," she blurted.

I sighed. "Yes and no. We have no evidence, no proof that Macey killed her father."

"That's why we need to go to her warehouse, search it, find the evidence."

It wasn't a stupid idea. Only right now, I was too lethargic to do anything other than breathe. "We'll go tonight. Too risky going in broad daylight. Look how that turned out at Keelan's."

She looked like she was about to argue, but Calder's truck pulling into the driveway had her leaping from her armchair to go and greet him. I stayed where I was, boneless. I'd managed to put the cup on the coffee table by my side before it slipped from my fingers, but I wasn't sure I could trust my legs to hold my weight should I try to stand. Just what was in her herbal remedy, anyway? Something potent, that's for sure.

"Hey." Calder stepped into the living room, sucking up all the oxygen.

I turned my head and smiled at him. "Hey."

"She's had an herbal tea," Doris said. "Do you want one?"

Calder eyed me, the half-empty cup, then Doris. "What's in it?"

"Something that dissolves your bones," I drawled, blinking slowly.

"In that case, no thank you, I need my bones today."

"Suit yourself." She sniffed. "I'll leave you kids to it. Gotta water the roses." She about-faced and left the room.

Calder called after her, "Keep your clothes on!"

He pulled my phone out of his pocket and handed it to me before sitting in the armchair Doris had vacated.

"Thought I'd return your phone. See how you're doing. Last night was… a lot."

I placed the phone next to my cup, not bothering to check for messages.

"You're right. It was a lot."

Several seconds passed in tense silence. "You're okay?"

He wasn't talking about my injuries. He was asking if I was okay with the discovery that Joshua Calder, Gravestone's one and only sheriff, was not the human I thought he was. That he was, in fact, a bear shifter. Did it change things? Not really. I couldn't very well cry foul when I was keeping my own secrets.

"I'm fine. *We're* fine. It's okay," I assured him. Truth be told, I was still getting my head around it, still processing, but I was adept at shoving things into little boxes and slamming the lids shut.

Calder cleared his throat. "I'm sorry to have to ask this…" He trailed off, eyes beseeching.

"Spit it out."

"I'm going to have to ask you to keep this quiet. What you saw last night is going to have to stay between us."

My eyes narrowed as I considered what he was asking. It was a no brainer, of course. Secrets were my bread and butter. What was one more?

"Sure. I get it." I mimed locking my lips closed and throwing away the key. "Your secret is safe with me."

He visibly relaxed, leaning back in his chair. "Thanks. You're taking all of this remarkably well."

I laughed. If only he knew. I'd been through way worse than this, seen way more surprising and disturbing things than the local sheriff shifting into a bear. Nope, this was nothing compared to my usual day-to-day.

"I have a question," I said.

"Shoot."

"What happened to Dino? Is he…?"

"Dead? No. But he's left town. His car was clocked running a red light in Corpus Christi a short while ago. I doubt he'll be bothering you again anytime soon."

"Good." That didn't mean Dino wouldn't be back, but next time he decided to break into my house, I'd be waiting, and I'd be better prepared.

"And Kerris? Any luck tying her back to Dino?"

"Ahhh, our illustrious mayor, as slippery as ever." He ran a hand around the back of his neck with a heavy sigh. I figured he'd had more than one run-in with Kerris Jones—the woman had a way of turning up, smelling of roses and getting her own way. My eyes narrowed. Maybe I'd look into that on the side. Because I had a strong suspicion the mayor was using magic to sway people, to get the votes she needed for her projects. Heck, I wouldn't be surprised if witchcraft wasn't behind her getting elected in the first place.

"I confronted her with the results of the handwriting analysis—which, as you suggested, confirmed that Kerris wrote the note we found in Cody's hand."

"And? What did she say?"

"She said that she may well have written the note

but that she didn't give it to anyone. She'd jotted it down when you first came to town because she wanted to drop by and welcome you to Gravestone. Officially."

Oh, she was good. Damn good. And Calder was right, as slippery as an eel. I told him as much. "You're right… she's good. Yes, she did visit, but it wasn't to welcome me to town. We'd already bumped into each other at River's. Oh, no, she dropped by to try and convince me to sell her my house."

"Which isn't illegal," he pointed out.

"No it is not. So what? She's claiming someone *stole* it from her desk?"

He inclined his head. "Affirmative. She claims it could have gotten scooped up with papers or that someone could have seen it on her desk and picked it up, that her office isn't locked and people are in and out all the time."

"Flimsy."

"And I can't use it to hold her. It would never stack up in court. We have to play this carefully. And smart."

I slumped in my chair. I'd really been hoping we'd be able to pin *something* on Kerris, but it wasn't looking likely. Calder must've felt my frustration, for he leaned over and patted my knee. I decided I liked it and laid my hand over his. In that split second, I made a decision I hoped I wouldn't live to regret.

"I got the puzzle box open," I breathed, leaning forward, keeping his hand pressed to my knee, feeling his fingers tense for the briefest of moments before relaxing.

He knew. I saw it in his eyes, the flash of understanding. He knew I was placing a lot of faith and trust in him—not enough to tell him my real identity, but it was a good first step. "And?" He glanced out the window, searching for Doris.

"Does she still have her clothes on?" I asked, not taking my eyes off him.

He nodded, lips curling up at the corners. "She does. Go ahead. What was in the box?"

"It has to stay between us. You can't put this in any report." If he wanted me to keep his secret, he'd have to keep one of mine.

"Agreed."

I told him about the soul stone, the implications it had for Gravestone, that I'd handed the puzzle box over to Keelan Moore this morning, minus the soul stone, which remained safely hidden. By the time I'd finished speaking, Calder was holding both of my hands in his and leaning in so close our foreheads were almost touching.

"You're aware Moore is working for the Arzan Brotherhood?" Calder warned, squeezing my hands.

I nodded. "I'm aware. Are you aware he's a vampire?"

Calder nodded. Damn. If only we'd compared notes earlier! "I'm worried about Doris," I confessed. "And this is based on a lot of *ifs*. If Keelan gets the puzzle box open sooner rather than later and discovers a rock instead of a soul stone, will he think Cody did the big ol' switch-a-roo? Or will he think it was me? And if he thinks that, he could easily compel Doris to tell him the truth because he knows he can't compel me."

"She knows?"

"Oh, yeah, she knows. And she's susceptible to his persuasion. I'm somehow immune."

Calder released one of my hands to gently touch my collarbone. "Could be something to do with this."

"My birthmark?" We both knew it wasn't a birthmark. The Algiz rune that was branded onto my skin as a form of protection was doing its job.

"Of course, the other option is that the soul stone had already been switched out when Cody acquired the puzzle box," Calder suggested. "All we have to do is plant that seed and allow that little piece of disinformation to circulate. Should Keelan return," he added.

"Smart. I like it." I grinned and flexed my fingers, the boneless feeling starting to recede. Thank goodness I hadn't drunk the whole cup of tea. I'd be passed out on the floor. "While we're exchanging intel, how about you share what you know about the murder weapon? What killed Cody Pendant?"

He didn't hesitate. "Coroner says it was a round, blunt object."

"Not a rock then. A tree branch?"

He shook his head. "Gold paint particulates were found in the wound, indicating it was something manufactured, not organic like a piece of wood. And there's nothing at the crime scene that matches, so the killer most likely took it with them when they left."

"And Macey? She's the only suspect we have left."

Calder huffed out a soft laugh. "Shoulda known the two of you were investigating."

"I love solving a good mystery in between baking bread," I admitted, keeping a straight face.

"Fine. After this, I'm heading out to interview Macey."

"Any evidence against her?"

"A partial fingerprint on the scrap of paper."

Everything kept coming back to the piece of paper with my name on it. "Do you think she could have killed her own father?"

He shrugged. "It's possible. We saw how he spoke to her. Maybe she was with him that night. They argued—again—and she just snapped. Killed him with whatever she had on hand."

I snapped my fingers. "We know Cody was into all sorts of shady deals. What if he was meeting a client that night, handing over something counterfeit or smuggled or whatever? Something that person didn't want to be seen buying. So, Macey goes with him to the handover because she's taking over the business…"

"And it all goes sideways," Calder finished. "Maybe Macey killed him. Maybe the client."

"But if it was the client, why let Macey live?"

"Because she was in on it? Or she got away."

We looked at each other, wide-eyed. Then Calder snapped his head around and stared out the window, his body alert.

"What is it?" I looked out the window, didn't see

anything other than Doris's beautiful garden in full bloom and blue skies for a change.

"It's Doris," he said, standing and crossing to the window, looking this way and that.

I surged to my feet in a panic, joining him. "What is it? Is she all right? Is she hurt?"

He shook his head. "She's gone."

CHAPTER
Nineteen

I followed Calder outside, confirming that the Impala was indeed missing. Crafty old witch. She must've rolled it out of the driveway so we wouldn't hear the engine.

"Any idea where she's gone? And why she felt the need to sneak off like that?" he asked, standing with his legs planted and hands on hips.

"I'll bet you ten bucks she's gone to visit Macey." Doris had been chomping at the bit to visit Macey and prove she was the murderer. I couldn't believe she'd go without me.

"I'm not going to take that bet." Calder heaved a breath, then pulled his keys from his pocket. "Come on, let's go find her before she gets herself into trouble."

My jaw dropped. "You're letting me come with you?" I'd felt for sure he'd make me stay behind and keep my nose out of it.

"The best way I can keep an eye on you is to keep you within eyeshot. Hop in."

I did as instructed, climbing into the passenger seat while trying not to take offense that he felt he needed to keep an eye on me. Though to be fair, I hadn't told Calder the whole truth, that I was a trained SIA agent who didn't require supervision. Plus, I'd be cutting off my nose to spite my face—I needed a ride, and he was it.

"So, where do you think Doris would go?" he asked, reversing out of the driveway. His truck had conveniently blocked the view of the Impala that had been parked next to it. Oh, but she was sneaky. I liked it. What I didn't like was that Doris didn't know she could be walking into danger. Macey was way more involved in her father's business than we gave her credit for.

"We were talking about searching the Pendants' storage unit on Thuruna Road. Our plan was to try and find the murder weapon first, without tipping Macey off."

"That's something, at least." Calder shot me a look. "But going in blindly, not knowing what you're looking for? That's why you should leave it to the professionals," he scolded.

I shrugged. I'd know what I was looking for when I found it, and this wasn't mine, nor Doris's, first rodeo. But Calder didn't need to know that. Not yet, anyway.

The storage facility was actually a shipping container. Doris's Impala was parked out front, and the doors to the container stood open. Calder pulled up next to Doris's car. "Stay here," he instructed as he climbed out and headed toward the container. I waited precisely five seconds before getting out and following. Calder heard me and turned, an exasperated look on his face. I smiled and winked, then my attention shifted. There was movement in the shipping container, and Macey appeared in the doorway. You'd think it would be a thousand degrees in the container yet standing there in a white sundress with her green hair braided, she looked as cool as a cucumber. And maybe a little calculating. Of Doris, there was no sign.

"Sheriff. Holly." Macey acknowledged us. "What can I do for you?"

"Where's Doris?" I blurted, before Calder could get a word out. He shot me a look that said *please be quiet*, only it was a lot less polite.

Macey jerked her thumb over her shoulder. "She's inside having a look around."

I strained my ears, trying to hear sounds of Doris doing exactly that, but it was eerily silent. "Mind if I join her?"

Calder rolled his eyes in an *I give up* gesture.

"By all means. Go right ahead." She stepped outside, allowing me to step into the container. I was right. It was hot in here. Within seconds, my skin was slick with sweat.

"Doris?" I called, making my way among the maze of boxes and furniture crammed into the container, stacked high, right up to the ceiling in places. I heard

Calder talking to Macey behind me, all official, but my attention was on finding Doris. I was worried Macey had done something to her.

The farther into the container I went, the dimmer it got, and the air was hot and thick. I tugged at the neckline of my T-shirt, already damp from the sheer amount of sweat. How could Macey stand to be in here? And why wasn't she sweating? I wondered if she were some sort of fire demon who loved the heat and thrived in such conditions when I stumbled across Doris, who was examining a jewelry box.

"Doris?"

She turned, guilt flashing across her face. "Oh, hi, Holly," she said loudly, then lowered her voice. "Sorry. You and Calder were all googly eyes at each other, so I figured I'd make myself scarce."

"You didn't have to do that. And we weren't being all googly eyes either," I protested, feeling my hot face grow even hotter.

"Potatoes, tomatoes," she brushed away my words. "Macey was already here, so I figured I'd ask if I could have a look at some of her wares—since I didn't get a chance to stop by their booth on Saturday."

I was impressed. "Smart."

Doris beamed. "Right?"

"How's it going, ladies? Find anything you like?" Macey said from behind us, making us both jump. Hand on my thundering heart, I spun to face her.

"You startled me. I didn't hear you."

She smiled, a smile that didn't reach her eyes.

"Sorry." She wasn't. I looked over her shoulder, searching for Calder. "Where's the sheriff?"

"He had to leave."

Really? So, whatever Macey had told him must have proved her innocence. I had to admit, I was a bit hurt that he'd left without a word. He must've figured I'd hitch a ride with Doris.

"So, tell us, Macey, what are your plans for all of this now that it's yours?"

"I'm sure you've heard that I'm selling the business to Keelan." Her tone was waspish, far from the sweet young woman I'd met at the market.

"But why?" Doris asked, genuinely curious.

Macey snorted, "Because this business had always been dad's dream. Not mine. But he was retiring, and I had my own plans. Plans that didn't involve doing this," she waved a hand around at the items stacked inside the shipping container, "for the rest of my life."

"What do you want to do?" I'd often wondered what I'd do if I couldn't work for the SIA anymore. Maybe open my own bakery?

"I want to go to Paris, France, and visit the Louvre."

I pursed my lips, only half surprised by her answer. Growing up around antiquities, I'd imagine you'd have to have some appreciation for art. "So, you're into art?"

"Yes."

I had a feeling she wasn't telling me the whole story, but then what did it matter what she planned to do with her life once she sold the business? I couldn't imagine it was going to net her much of a profit. As far as I could tell, Cody Pendant was not a big fish, and if the stock in the container was anything to go by, there was not a lot of value in it. No, Cody Pendant made his money by *acquiring* black market occult items. The whole antiquities business was a cover, nothing more.

"I hear you gave Keelan the puzzle box," Macey said, studying her nails. "Smart move."

"Really? You heard that? Who from?"

"Keelan dropped in to say goodbye. Now that he had what was *rightfully* his, he had no reason to hang around."

I bristled a little at her dig but let it slide. "That reminds me. I was in the mayor's office and noticed she has a puzzle box very similar to the one you sold me. Did your dad get it for her?"

"Dad did a lot of business with the mayor." Macey nodded. "I don't recall a puzzle box specifically, but it's highly likely. You know," she leaned in and lowered her voice, "as far as I'm concerned, the mayor is a person of interest. In Dad's murder."

"Oh?"

"Mmm hmm. I saw her that night, meeting with Dino Cittadino. She handed him something, and he shoved it in his pocket. Only neither of them noticed that it fell out. I waited till they'd gone, then picked it up."

"What was it?" Doris asked, picking up a ceramic vase and turning it this way and that.

"It was a note, with your name and address written on it." She looked me dead in the eye, as if expecting this to be news to me. Only it wasn't. I'd already heard Dino and Kerris talking about this very thing. "Kerris Jones has plans for you," Macey continued ominously. "You'd best watch your back." That explained why Calder had found Macey's fingerprint on the note. She'd picked it up. But how had it gotten into Cody's hand?

I cocked my head, wondering if Macey had paid any attention whatsoever to my appearance, for surely any fool and their dog could see I'd been involved in an altercation recently, what with the scrapes and bruises marring my flesh, not to mention the dressing covering the stitches in my shoulder. Although, to be fair, they were covered by the red T-shirt.

I watched the young woman, the one who I'd initially thought so naïve, downtrodden by her father. But now I saw a glimpse of what River had told me. There was more to Macey Pendant than met the eye, a cynical, hard layer to the softness she projected. Maybe she wasn't so much of a victim after all.

"You wouldn't happen to know what that plan is, would you?" I asked.

She shifted her gaze over my shoulder, as if to check that no one was approaching, then shot a look at Doris before bringing her attention back to me. "Look, you didn't hear it from me, but word is the mayor hired Dino to scare you into leaving town."

"Ha!" Doris snorted. "Fat chance of that."

Macey frowned. "You don't believe me?"

"No, not that." Doris waved a statue at her. "If

Kerris Jones, our illustrious mayor, thinks she can scare Holly into leaving, she'd better think again." Doris turned to me. "It's like the woman has never met you."

I forced a laugh. "Right?" But Doris was missing the point. How did Macey know all of this if she wasn't involved? Whatever went down between Dino, the mayor, and her father, Macey was up to her neck in it.

"Well, ladies, it's been fun chatting." Her tone said it hadn't. "But I'm sorry, it's time for you to go. I'm locking up now."

"Oh." Doris sounded disappointed, and I figured she'd forgotten we weren't here to shop, we were here to snoop.

That was when I heard it. A groan from outside. Doris heard it too. "What's that?" She was standing between me and Macey and made a move to go check out the sound we'd heard when Macey suddenly grabbed her, an arm across her chest, a knife to her throat. Doris squeaked, caught off guard.

"What are you doing?" I asked, glancing around, trying to find a suitable weapon to defend myself with.

"Ha!" she sneered, tightening her hold on Doris. "Don't act all innocent with me. I know you know."

"Know what?" Doris asked.

"That I killed Dad," she spat, eyes sparkling with anger.

"Oh." Doris fluttered her eyelashes, totally wasted because Macey was behind her and couldn't see. "So, it *was* you?"

"Like you didn't know. Why else are you here? And you brought the sheriff."

That was the groan I'd heard. She'd incapacitated Calder somehow, only he was coming around. Which meant that a) he wasn't dead and b) she'd had no intentions of allowing us to leave the container alive.

Keeping my knees bent and my eyes on Macey, I felt blindly behind me, my fingers finding one of the dozen miniature statues I'd noticed in a box earlier. I lifted it, testing the weight. Small but weighty. Not ideal, but it would do the job. A swift blow to the temple should render her unconscious—even as I thought it, I knew I had the answer.

"You killed him with one of these, didn't you?" I held up a replica of the statue in the town square, of Marilla and her baby, Earendil. The statue was covered in gold paint and secured on a round base. I bet the coroner could match it perfectly to the wound on Cody's skull and the gold fragments to the paint on the statue.

"He got what he had coming," Macey spat, her grip on Doris relaxing a fraction. "He thought he was such a big deal, a big player, when he was nothing but a small-minded hick, a nobody."

She was on a roll, cheeks flushed, eyes crazed as she spouted her hatred for her father. "He thinks he was so smart smuggling fairy dust in these?" She jerked her head toward the statues behind me. "It was *my* idea. Mine! Did I get any credit? Did I get a cut of the proceeds? Of course not," she scoffed. "He was greedy and selfish, and I'd kill him again if I could."

"So, what happened? The night you killed him," I clarified. "You followed him to a deal and just… killed him?" So cold-blooded.

She rolled her eyes. "No. It was *our* first deal. For once, I was allowed to attend—since I was taking over the business and all. He acted like I had no clue. That I wouldn't know how a deal is meant to go down when I've been doing my own deals behind his back since I was fifteen. Moron. Anyway, to answer your question, no, I wasn't actually intending to kill him. My plan had always been to wait him out, get him to retire, get control of the business, and sell it. Use the proceeds to bankroll a new life far away from him. I couldn't wait to see the look on his face when I sold his precious business. It's what kept me going all these years.

"It was stupid really." Her voice lowered, her mind lost in the past as she relived the night she murdered her father. "We were waiting at the town square for our client. Cody thought it was hilarious to hand over a statue of Marilla beneath the real statue. Anyway, I'd had one hand in my pocket and when I pulled it out, the scrap of paper I'd seen Dino drop—the one I picked up and shoved in my pocket—fell out. Dad saw it, picked it up, and got the wrong end of the stick. He thought I was involved in the job out on you, and he was mad I'd get into bed with the mayor, that she'd have something to hold over my head forever. He wouldn't listen when I told him that I wasn't involved, and he just went on and on about how useless I was. What a disappointment. The next thing I know, he's on the ground, and I'm standing over him with a bloody statue."

"And your client? What did they think when they turned up to a murder scene?"

She shrugged. "They didn't. I sent a message saying the deal was off. They never turned up."

"Who was your client?" Doris asked.

"Wouldn't you like to know?" she sneered. Removing the knife from Doris's throat, she pointed it at me. "You. You are in the middle of this entire mess. If you hadn't come to town, the mayor wouldn't want you gone, wouldn't have hired Dino, who wouldn't have dropped that stupid note. And all your meddling has led the police here, to me."

"What can I say? I'm good like that." I gave Doris a slight nod, and without hesitation, she rammed her elbow into Macey's solar plexus, then reached up, grabbed Macey's braids, and tossed her up and over her shoulder. Macey landed with a resounding thud, flat on her back in front of me, having somersaulted over Doris. The knife slipped from her hand and skidded across the floor. Doris leaped for it while I sat on Macey, my knees on her arms, while she wheezed and struggled to catch her breath, trying to work out what had just happened.

"Freeze, police!" Calder staggered out from behind some boxes, gun drawn, only to lower it when he caught sight of me sitting on Macey and Doris brandishing the knife. Blood trickled from his temple.

"Are you okay?" I asked.

"She sure can pack a punch." He flinched as his fingers explored the wound. "Caught me by surprise."

"Yeah, that's her specialty." I hopped off Macey while Calder slapped on a pair of cuffs and arrested her.

"I reckon if you spray this lot with luminol, you'll find your murder weapon," I told him, indicating the box full of Marilla statues. I lowered my voice. "Also, you may want to check 'em for fairy dust. She and Cody had a little smuggling ring going on."

He nodded, then dragged Macey outside, Doris and I following behind.

"Are you all right?" I asked Doris. "You shouldn't have come here on your own. That was dangerous."

"It all worked out okay in the end. We got our killer." She beamed, her cheeks flushed, her eyes sparkling. "Now it's time to celebrate."

I'd been on the receiving end of Doris's celebrations before. It was bad for my liver. "I still have laundry to do," I hedged.

"Come on, spoilsport." Doris flung her arm around my waist. "Just one drink."

"Okay, fine," I relented, knowing she wouldn't leave it alone until I did. "One drink."

CHAPTER
Twenty

Who knew doing laundry could be fun? While Doris shoved clothes into the washer with total disregard for color sorting or delicates, Flynn ran around sporting a crown made out of tinsel and a little red cape. Where he'd gotten either of them, I did not know. I suspected Doris had magicked them up for him, but he was loving himself sick right now, and it was the most adorable thing I'd ever seen.

"Hey." I lifted my glass, narrowly avoiding sloshing red wine onto the floor. "I just remembered. The book."

"What book?" Doris picked up the bottle of wine to refill her glass, only the bottle was empty. She frowned at it. "This bottle is faulty," she grumbled.

"The book Casey found in John Smith's wall." I staggered to the living room where I'd dropped my backpack earlier and retrieved the leather-bound book before weaving my way back to the dining room—base camp for our celebration because it was adjacent to the laundry, and I was insistent on washing my clothes.

Doris had found another bottle of wine and was in the process of removing the cork. It flew across the room with a pop, and Flynn took off in hot pursuit, looking like a miniature super hero with his cape flowing behind him.

Doris took a hefty gulp of wine straight from the bottle. "Apologies for the backwash," she said, refilling her glass. "So, what's in the book? A story?"

I shook my head, putting my hand over my glass when Doris went to top it up. "Nuh-uh. I've had enough."

"Pft," she sniffed, flopping into a chair and waving her glass around. "Go on then, read me this story."

"It's not a story. It's a journal. Of sorts. There are sketches and notes and lists of names, and something I noticed earlier—the handwriting changes. I think this," I pointed to the book, "was handed down. Maybe from John Smith's parents to him."

"Like an heirloom?"

"Yes! Exactly." I lowered my voice. "I also think this is what people have been breaking into my house for."

"Huh?"

"That intruder? They were upstairs in the master bedroom—the only thing in that room was the bookcase. We thought the break-in was something to do with the puzzle box, but I think that was a coincidence. The intruder was searching the bookcase for *this!*"

Flynn returned with the cork tucked under his arm.

Standing next to my wineglass, he was nodding and squeaking. "Is that right, Flynn? Did you see the intruder actually searching the bookcase?"

He shrugged, helpful as ever.

"A quick glance would have told anyone the puzzle box wasn't on the bookshelf. No searching required. But if you were looking for an old book, where would you look?"

"The bookcase," Doris slurred.

"Exactly!"

She waved her glass at me, red wine sloshing over the rim. "So, what's so important about the book?"

I shrugged, turning my attention back to the open pages. "Get this," I said. "It mentions the Shadow Binder Covenant—isn't that what Denise Hurt was involved with? And something about a Shadowfall Amulet." The words were starting to blur, and my eyes grew heavier and heavier until I rested my head on my arm and closed them for the briefest of moments.

I'm not sure how long I slept, but when I awoke, my face was stuck to the journal. Carefully peeling it off and wiping away the residual drool, I looked over at Doris, who was passed out across from me, head resting on her folded arms on the dining room table. The washing machine had finished its cycle and was silent, and Flynn was spread-eagle on his back, snoring. Narrowing my eyes, I leaned in, examining his whiskers. Sneaky rat. He'd been into the wine, residual traces of it caught in the fur around his mouth. At least he hadn't puked this time.

Sitting up, I stretched, easing the kinks out of my back and neck, then turned my attention back to the book. Now that I was sober, or sober enough that the words weren't a jumble on the page, I noticed something I'd missed before. On a blank page, in different but familiar handwriting, were the words:

Choices made long ago bear grave consequences in this age.

A shiver danced up my spine. I recognized the handwriting. It was the same as the mysterious note left at my house, the one I hadn't written and Doris denied writing, the last time we'd celebrated catching a killer. Shaking my head, I figured Doris was playing games with me and slammed the book closed before heading outside to hang out my laundry. It'd dry in no time, and then I could finally get changed out of the leopard print leggings and red Christmas tee that were uniquely Doris Shutt.

That's the end of book two~thanks for reading!
Are you ready to continue Holly's journey in book three,
What the Hex:
www.JaneHinchey.com/Gravestone/what-the-hex

AFTERWORD

Thank you for reading, if you enjoyed **Fur the Hex of it**, please consider leaving a review. You can find a complete list of my books, including series and reading order on my website at:

www.JaneHinchey.com

Also, if you'd like to sign up to receive emails with the latest news, exclusive offers, and more, you can do that here:

www.JaneHinchey.com/subscribe

And finally, I'd love to invite you to join my **VIP Readers group** where you get exclusive access to me, the opportunity to win one of the monthly signed paperback giveaways, join in live videos, get sneak peeks at works in progress and so much more.

www.JaneHinchey.com/LittleDevils

Thank you so much for taking a chance and reading my book - I do this for you.

xoxo

Jane

The guest list for the shifter party Kristina Gates is catering has just turned into a suspect list—for murder.

When Ted McNeil is found dead at a high society event, it looks at first like he choked on one of Kristina's cupcakes. But it soon becomes evident that foul play was involved. The cupcake was poisoned.

Kristina's determination to salvage her reputation and learn the truth launches her quest to appease the Witches' Council and avoid a life sentence in the pokey. With the help of her fae friends and sexy Watcher Ben Hoffman, she untangles a web of lies that threaten her very existence.

Faced with a mysterious foe, a family of tight-lipped shifters, and a competitor who would stop at nothing to put her out of business, Kristina realizes nothing is as it seems and the shadows hold secrets that some would kill to keep.

Get a copy of Cupcakes & Curses for FREE as a thank you for joining my newsletter! Sign up here: www.JaneHinchey.com/subscribe

About Jane

Jane Hinchey delivers snort-worthy cozy mysteries and sizzling paranormal romances that grab readers from the get-go. With tenacious heroines, lovable sidekicks, and heroes who are more than just a pretty face, her books are an irresistible mix of humor, magic, and heart. From witches cracking cases to vampires in love, she offers an adventure where the extraordinary is the norm and love bites in the best way.

Find Jane here: www.janehinchey.com

facebook.com/janehincheyauthor

instagram.com/janehincheyauthor

amazon.com/Jane-Hinchey/e/B0193449MI

bookbub.com/authors/jane-hinchey

goodreads.com/jane_hinchey